PRAISE FOR T
REINHARDT M

"This is a wonderful introduction to Roxy and her new friends. The environment is delightful. The details add wonderful depth. I enjoyed it greatly."

"Roxy is a delight & I thoroughly enjoyed her debut."

"I read your book until the wee hours last night.... couldn't put it down!!"

"All the food made me very hungry and really wanting to visit New Orleans!"

"Absolutely loved it!!!"

"You've done a great job. Truly. This one shines."

"I just want you to know how much I like Roxy. She makes me smile."

"Loved the book, looking forward to the next installment. I think you've got a winner!"

"I like Roxy and her new friends and look forward to more books including them."

"Love Roxy's posse."

"What a great book!"

"Loved it!"

"Excellent characterization."

"I need to tell you that you have a winner here."

"I'm enjoying this new series immensely. Congratulations on the start of another great series."

"Loved your new series!"

"The story was fantastic!"

"Storyline and character development is easy flowing, interesting, and really holds the reader's interest. Overall a great new series to look forward to!"

"Loved the book, looking forward to the next installment. I think you've got a winner!"

MARDI GRAS MADNESS

BOOKS IN THE ROXY REINHARDT MYSTERIES

Visit the link below for all my large print editions:

www.alisongolden.com/large-print

Mardi Gras Madness

New Orleans Nightmare

Louisiana Lies

Cajun Catastrophe

COLLECTIONS

(regular print only)

Books 1-3

Mardi Gras Madness

New Orleans Nightmare

Louisiana Lies

The characters and events portrayed in this book are fictitious. Any similarity to real persons, living or dead is coincidental and not intended by the author.

Published by Mesa Verde Publishing
P.O. Box 1002
San Carlos, CA 94070

ISBN: 979-8863856216

"A book is a device to ignite the imagination."
- Alan Bennett -

MARDI GRAS MADNESS

ALISON GOLDEN

HONEY BROUSSARD

"Your emails seem to come on days when I need to read them because they are so upbeat."
- Linda W -

For a limited time, you can get the first books in each of my series - *Chaos in Cambridge, Hunted* (exclusively for subscribers - not available anywhere else), *The Case of the Screaming Beauty, and Mardi Gras Madness* - plus updates about new releases, promotions, and other Insider exclusives, by signing up for my mailing list at:

https://www.alisongolden.com/roxy

CHAPTER ONE

"WHAT IS *WRONG* with you?" the man said.

Roxy blinked repeatedly to get her view of the world to clear. As it was, everything blurred with unshed tears. The call center desks warped as the fluid in her eyes distorted everything, stretching out desks and squeezing people until it all looked as wrong as it felt. *Please don't let me cry . . . please don't let me cry.*

"Sir," Roxy said, praying her voice wouldn't shake, "I have to remind you to remain non-abusive in your interactions with customer service." She adjusted her headset and swallowed hard. "It would be easier for us to troubleshoot your washing machine problems if you were a little calmer."

"I am calm!" the man at the other end of the line shouted, adding a strong curse word for good measure.

"Okay," said Roxy, just about holding it together enough that her voice didn't tremble. "Just a second, please." She hit the "hold" button and let out a long breath trying to calm herself. What she didn't expect was a little sob to escape, too.

Jade had heard and turned around with a nasty gleeful look on her face. "Are you *crying*, Roxy?" she asked, her eyes shining. Straightening up in her seat, Roxy tucked her blonde flyaways behind her ears.

"No," Roxy said quickly. Some days this job felt so much like high school. It was as though bullies picked on her, sneered at her, and followed her around. She always seemed to have to "protect" herself from Jade, as well as Chloe, the girl in front who was mercifully taking what seemed a long, drawn-out technical call.

Roxy tried to take no notice. All she wanted to do was go to the office each morning, work hard, save her money, go home and spend the evening snuggling on the couch with her boyfriend Ryan and fluffy white princess cat Nefertiti. Was that too much to ask?

Apparently it was, as Jade and Chloe always seemed to have something smart and cutting to say.

In Chloe's case, it was often cloaked as a "compliment."

"Oh, Roxy, your hair looks nice today. At least, it looks *so* much better than it did yesterday," or "Oh, Roxy, I wish I had a figure like yours. All the men chase after me because of my curves, and it's just *so* annoying."

Roxy was short, only five-feet-two. She had a slim, small-boned figure with which she was mostly at peace. But she was frequently carded and even mistaken for her boyfriend's much younger sister, despite being 24.

Roxy was generally secure enough in herself to recognize these young women, her co-workers, as insecure and rude and their "compliments" as silliness. However, today she wasn't able to let their comments roll off her back quite so easily. She took a deep breath. In truth it felt like everything in her life was falling apart, and she had no clue how to patch it back together again.

Always one to try and look on the bright side at times like these, she would tell herself, "At least I still have my savings." Having grown up in a semi-rural, impoverished home in Ohio, this money that she had put aside was very important to her. The cushion of money made her feel so *safe*.

Roxy didn't make all that much as a call center customer service rep, but she religiously transferred a couple hundred dollars into her savings account each month. It meant bringing in sandwiches and coffee in a flask instead of buying them from the store next door like everyone else, but it was worth it for the glorious feeling of security. Heck, it meant coming to her miserable call center job day in and day out, but if that's what it took, that's what it took. She would pay the price of 50 percent boredom, 50 percent stress for the peace of mind she felt when she checked her bank balance—something she did at *least* once a day. Seeing that dollar amount next to her name was thrilling to Roxy.

But not even her nest egg could save her from her other Big Problem. Ryan, her tall, dark, six-foot-five boyfriend, was slipping away. No, he was *wrenching* himself away. No matter what Roxy did, he was ruder and more distant—saying more and more hurtful things as the days went by. It wasn't his raised voice that hurt her so much; it was the look in his eyes. All the warmth had gone. He looked through her like she was a complete stranger. Her eyes welled up again.

She suddenly remembered her abusive customer at the end of the phone. She pressed the "hold" button to go back to the call but got nothing but a *beeeeeep* on the other end. He'd already hung up. Roxy flopped her head forward into her hands and swallowed. She'd give anything not to cry here.

Anything. The customer would call back and report her for leaving him on hold for so long, and her supervisor would dock her pay instantly, she just knew it.

Angela, her boss, was a cold, hard woman who prided herself on being "no-nonsense" with her employees, which in this case meant she was a real witch. Any little mistake, she docked pay. Didn't meet your call target for the day? Docked pay. Got to your desk one minute late? Docked pay. If anyone got sick or pregnant, she treated them like they'd made a terrible, unworthy choice and were exaggerating their symptoms.

Roxy felt her phone vibrate in her bag. She knew it would be Ryan—he was the only one who called her. Preferring a quiet, almost silent life, she had very few friends, and her mom never called. She'd never met her father, so it couldn't possibly be him. Roxy felt a huge urge to reach down and check her phone surreptitiously. Cell phones, however, were strictly forbidden in the office. Getting caught using it one time was a fineable offense. Twice? Instantaneous termination of employment.

Roxy valued her job too much to check her phone, but her mind ran wild trying to work out why Ryan might have texted her. Was it a "sorry for being a jerk, honey bun, let's move on," kind of text? Or, much more likely, a variation on "you're so unambitious, and you're holding my life back." The latter seemed to be his latest complaint.

Roxy couldn't ruminate for too long, however, because the phone on her desk rang again—a new customer service call to take. "Good afternoon, you're through to Modal Appliances, Inc. My name's Roxy. How may I help you today?"

CHAPTER TWO

"OH, HELLO," THE voice of an elderly lady said. "I've just bought a new washing machine, and I can't work out all these complicated buttons. Do you think you could help me with that?"

"Of course, ma'am," Roxy said with a forced smile. "Do you know what model of machine you bought by any chance?"

"No, dear, I'm afraid I don't."

"No problem," Roxy said. "Let me walk you through how to find that out. There's a special sticker on the back of the machine."

"Oh, thank you," the old lady said. "That would be very kind of you, Roxy."

"You're so welcome."

Roxy's favorite calls were those where she could help people who were polite and respectful, even grateful, and she dared to believe that perhaps her day was looking up just the tiniest bit.

But then she caught sight of Angela, her supervisor, marching over. From where Roxy sat, it didn't look like Angela was using her "We're-Hitting-Targets-And-I'm-Giving-You-A-Huge-Bonus" walk. It was more like "I'm-On-The-Warpath-And-About-To-Give-You-Hell." Angela's eyes locked onto Roxy and didn't leave her face.

Jade, even though she was on a call, noticed Angela storm by and turned to flash her eyes wide at Roxy, evidently delighted by the promise of impending drama. Roxy's fingers began to shake ever so slightly as Angela came to a stop next to Roxy's desk and towered over her, folding her arms. Roxy looked up, but Angela flapped at her dismissively, signaling that she should get back to the call.

Roxy pulled up the relevant manual on her screen and prepared to talk the elderly woman through the buttons on her machine. Roxy couldn't concentrate what with Angela looming over her, however, and she made a couple of mistakes as she explained. She sputtered and wondered if Angela had noticed. What was she thinking? Of course, Angela had noticed.

"Thank you, dear," the elderly woman said at the end of the call. "I *think* I understand now."

"I'm glad to hear it," Roxy said. She tried to put good-natured friendliness into the call like she always did, but she was so anxious that it came out all rushed and a tad insincere. "If you have any more questions please feel free to call us again. Thank you for calling Modal Appliances, Inc. Have a nice day." Roxy spun her chair around to face Angela.

Her supervisor launched into a lecture before Roxy even had the time to blink. "You do know I've just had some idiot yelling at me, telling me that you had *hung up on him* and that he was going to complain about Modal Appliances' customer service to anyone who would listen because we don't value our customers."

"Oh . . ." Roxy took a deep breath and looked up at Angela. She tried to meet her eyes, but it was hard. Angela's gaze felt like a pair of lasers boring into her. "Well, I didn't hang up on him. I just put him on hold for a moment, to . . ."

"To what?" Angela exploded!

"To collect myself," Roxy bravely continued. She *hated* confrontation. "Because he was being abusive."

"To *collect* yourself," Angela said with a mocking smile. "Oh, well that's just swell. Are you sure you're cut out for this job, Roxy?"

Roxy felt a lump in her throat. It was such an unfair question. She had consistently met her targets and often had customers tell her how kind and helpful she was. An elderly gentleman had even once said that she had made his week. "Yes" was all Roxy could come out with.

Angela snorted. "Not convincing. Pack your stuff."

"Wh . . . what?"

"Take your bag and your lunchboxes and go," Angela said, pointing towards the door at the end of the corridor between the cubicles.

"Go . . . you mean, like, forever?"

Angela was already walking away. "I haven't decided yet. I'll call you if I want you to come back."

"But . . ." Roxy began. Angela was already too far away to hear her.

Now the world *did* begin to distort and warp with her tears. She packed her lunch things into her handbag and took her favorite pen—a purple fluffy thing with a cat on it that wrote as smooth as anything—from the desktop. There was nothing else of hers there. She didn't look at Jade or Chloe, but that didn't stop her from hearing them gossip about her.

"About time, if you ask me," Chloe said, in a whisper that was much too loud to be tactful.

"Maybe we can finally get someone hired who actually fits in."

"Right?" Jade said, "And, hopefully someone with more fashion sense."

Roxy knew they were being snarky and mean, but that didn't stop their comments from stinging. She swung her bag over her shoulder and strode down the aisle of the office determined not to look at anyone. She kept her head high as if she were full of confidence, and, thankfully, she made it to the door without stumbling in her kitten heels as she had sometimes done in the past. However, a tear did slide down her cheek, and she had to quickly wipe it away.

Once in her car—the smallest, most reliable car Roxy had been able to find without putting herself into debt—she had a good cry. Tears streamed down her cheeks as she bent forward to turn on the ignition. She even had a little wail as she drove back to the apartment she shared with Ryan. She hadn't cried in so incredibly long that it felt weirdly good to do so. All her sadness, disappointment, humiliation—and yes, anger—gushed from beneath her long, dark eyelashes in watery rivulets that she couldn't have stopped if she'd tried.

As Roxy climbed the stairs to her apartment, she paused in the dingy stairwell. How should she be? Should she wipe all her tears away and put on a brave face? Maybe then Ryan wouldn't think of her as such a drag. Or should she allow herself to cry in front of him so he could see how upset all this was making her? Then, perhaps, he'd find an iota of emotion—preferably a supportive one—and wrap her up in his strong arms like he used to.

But Roxy didn't know what he would do anymore. She felt like she didn't know *him* anymore. She still really wanted to. She had this desperate urge to reconnect with him, to rekindle their spark. But how? She'd tried pretty much everything. And this on top of her dismissal made her so unsure that she couldn't be certain of the ground beneath her feet.

Roxy looked at herself in her makeup mirror and scrubbed at her blotchy face with a tissue. Her lashes clumped but the light hitting the surface of her moist eyes made them shine. One of her gold stud earrings was missing.

Roxy was an attractive young woman. A few times throughout her life she had been told that she was beautiful, a compliment she vigorously denied. Her insecurity made her shake in the face of such approval. She would blush furiously.

But, in truth, her pale skin was like alabaster while her bone structure was delicate. She had deep blue, heavy-lidded, almond-shaped eyes that sat atop a neat, upturned nose. She had a full, small mouth. As she looked in the mirror she could see that her nose was red and her lips were swollen, both a result of her tears.

Roxy's oval face and fine features were accentuated by her short, blonde hair. The length of it was one of the few things upon which Roxy stood firm. While her boyfriend objected to her hair being so short, Roxy detested spending time styling it. The result was a "wash and go" cut that was perfect for her, even though the "swish" that Ryan craved was lacking.

Roxy patted down her plain white T-shirt, and beige skirt, flattening out the wrinkles and turned the key in the lock of her apartment door. She felt numb. Nefertiti, her cat with a cute squashed-up face and an abundance of pristine white fur, was waiting for her in the hallway as usual.

"Hello, my sweet girl," Roxy said, giving the cat a rub under her chin. She straightened up. "Ryan?"

Ryan worked as a graphic designer from the comfort of their couch and was mostly home, but Roxy's voice echoed around the apartment. There was no reply. She headed into the bedroom to see if he was asleep. He wasn't there. Her heart dropped. She saw the closet. His side was empty, the hangers askew.

Roxy dove into her purse for her phone remembering that she hadn't yet read his text message. Her heart hammered.

Bye, Roxy. I'm moving in with my new girlfriend. Thanks for the fun times.

CHAPTER THREE

ROXY DIDN'T GET dinner. She didn't even change out of her work clothes. Usually, the first thing she'd do when she got in was shower, slip into some clean pajamas and fluffy cat slippers that looked quite like Nefertiti, and pad around the apartment for the rest of the evening. But today, Roxy simply crashed onto the bed and fell asleep fully clothed, with Nefertiti curled up beside her.

Ten hours later—as if it were the next moment —Roxy woke up in the same position that she had collapsed into the previous night. For a glorious moment or two, she enjoyed the golden morning sunlight streaming through the blinds and the feeling of wellbeing that her good, long sleep had given her, but then reality came crashing down. Ryan wasn't there. Ryan wasn't in her *life*. And she didn't even know if she had a job to go to.

Her mind started running. Would she have to dip into her savings? She could barely afford this apartment on her own *with* her job, let alone without it. Back when they had first rented it, she'd preferred a far more modest place so she could save even more of her paycheck. But Ryan had picked out this sleek one-bedroom, wooden-floored, white-walled apartment, and she'd have gone along with pretty much anything to make him happy. Now she'd gotten used to it.

Roxy's mind continued to race. What if she *had* lost her job? Where would she live? How would she eat? In her mind's eye, she could see it all too clearly—her savings spent, her car sold, the money from that spent too. Next she'd be destitute, on the street, cold and dirty with no one to care for or about her. Roxy's heart began to beat more quickly.

But then again, what if Angela did ask her back? What should she do? Sink deeper and deeper into this black hole of misery where her life crumbled to nothingness as Jade and Chloe looked on and laughed? As Angela tormented her day after day? As customers called up to curse at her for their washing machine woes? After all that, she'd come home to an empty apartment where Nefertiti would be the only ray of light in her otherwise dismal existence. None of the available options sounded good.

Nefertiti must have padded out of the room during the night, leaving the bed empty. Roxy rolled over onto her side, feeling thoroughly miserable and having talked herself into a depression as deep as the Grand Canyon. It was at times like these that she wished she had a friend, a true friend, someone who really understood her. Sure, there were a couple of people from school that she messaged on Facebook now and then, and one or two women from her old job that she sometimes went out with on the weekend. But she had no one who she could ugly-cry to on the phone and with whom she could share her worries.

Eventually, Roxy swallowed her tears, and with no phone call from Angela forthcoming, she moped around the house. Days like this called for a huge tub of ice cream, but she didn't have any in the freezer, and the thought of going to the store to buy some seemed to demand the amount of energy required to climb Mount Everest. The idea of *seeing* anyone felt horrifying.

Roxy sprawled out on the couch, arranging herself around Nefertiti's curled-up, white, fluffy softness and flipped through TV stations. There were Lifetime movies and some others she hadn't heard of, but a Tuesday morning didn't exactly get top programming. She tried to settle down to watch a *Dr. Phil*—anything—but neither her mind nor her body would settle, and she felt like launching the remote at the TV set. This was so unlike her that she startled herself.

Roxy sighed and went to the kitchen. She shoved a six-pack of yogurts from the refrigerator into the freezer hoping that would be an adequate substitute for ice cream. She purposefully walked back out of the kitchen before she leaned against the doorframe. "Oh, what's the point, Nefertiti?" Roxy said. But she could see from her place at the doorway that even the cat was ignoring her. Nefertiti was sitting bolt upright, staring at the TV.

"Hey," Roxy said with her first little smile of the day. Nefertiti looked so human as she sat on the sofa watching television, it made Roxy laugh. "What's so interesting, Nef?" Roxy stepped forward into the living room and turned to look at the screen.

"Oh . . ." she said. She watched the bright colors of a carnival flash up. The weirdest feeling overcame her—a feeling she'd never had before. She sat down beside Nefertiti; her eyes now glued to the screen. "Oh . . ." she said again. It was like she was watching something she'd seen or been a part of before, almost like nostalgia for something she'd never really known but knew about instinctively.

Roxy watched as carnival dancers spun and flashed their bright costumes, revelers packing the streets. She watched women in skimpy bright outfits, their bodies painted, twirling and dancing and laughing and looking *so* carefree. That was one thing Roxy wished she could be, carefree.

"Taste real life," a woman's voiceover on the commercial said. "Taste real culture. Taste Mardi Gras in New Orleans. We're waiting for you." The pounding sound of drums in the background matched the pounding of Roxy's heart.

Once the commercial had ended and an ad for some kind of drug had started, Roxy let out a little breath like *she'd* been dancing among the bright colors and booming drums. "Well," she breathed, looking at Nefertiti. She trailed off not quite knowing what to say. How could you explain *that* feeling? And why had Nefertiti been so interested? The fluffy cat sat back down again and curled up on the couch. Sinking back into her sleepy zone, she purred just a little.

Roxy felt baffled and, all of a sudden, not depressed at all.

She began tickling Nefertiti under her chin, and before she could stop it, a new, slightly scandalous idea was forming in her head.

"No, you couldn't *possibly,*" Roxy said to herself out loud. But a huge smile was spreading over her face. "Not sensible Roxy. She'd *never* do that." But talking the idea down only served to make a new rebellious streak in her gain strength. She got up feeling like a new person, full of energy, and sauntered over to the bedroom to get her laptop.

"All right," Roxy said, mentally preparing herself for what lay ahead. She threaded her fingers together and pushed her palms out in a stretch. She bobbed her head from side to side like a boxer preparing to enter the ring. "Okay." Butterflies danced in her stomach, but it felt thrilling rather than nerve-wracking. "I'm going to *do this.*"

She placed her fingertips on the keyboard, typed a few words, and pressed "Return."

CHAPTER FOUR

"HAVE I COMPLETELY and utterly lost my mind?" Roxy said to Nefertiti. She almost couldn't believe what she was doing. She had nearly had a panic attack when she realized that she was eating into her savings for the first time *ever*. The bus she was traveling in had been at a service station at the time. Now, Roxy poked her finger into Nefertiti's travel box, trying unsuccessfully to stroke her. "Have I gone totally crazy?"

The middle-aged lady across the aisle from Roxy clearly thought so by the look she shot her, though in fairness that was probably because Roxy had prattled on to Nefertiti constantly about all kinds of nonsense for the past three hours.

For her part, Roxy couldn't believe that she was now over 800 miles away from her home state of Ohio. She hadn't *ever* been that far before. The furthest she'd ventured was to visit some of Ryan's family in the Chicago suburbs.

That had been an uncomfortable visit. It was the first time she'd met Ryan's mom, who kept calling him, "My little Ry-Ry," waiting on him hand and foot, and undermining Roxy at every opportunity. She had made snide little "jokes" about her son's girlfriend, and Ryan had laughed along.

Roxy drifted into silence as she stared out the window as Alabama raced by. Her heart hurt a little. Life had changed so quickly. She thought she had been so *happy*—with Ryan, with her job, with her cozy life, with her cute apartment that she'd now given notice on, and with her little rusty car that she'd sold just before she left. All of the money went into her savings account, of course. But had she really been satisfied and content with her life? The overwhelming feeling Roxy got as she whizzed down the country to the South was *No, she had not*!

Roxy felt free now in a way she never had before. Her tension was easing. Her disappointing memories were disappearing in the rearview mirror of the bus. She was breaking into smiles more easily, and she alternately tapped her feet as she managed her pent-up energy. Roxy had been gone for fewer than 18 hours.

Perhaps leaving it all behind for a while wasn't going to be as hard as she thought. In a month she'd have to find somewhere to live and somewhere to work. Her new life wouldn't be one long Mardi Gras, but that was okay. When Roxy's pessimistic thoughts threatened to break through her excitement, she calmed herself with a lot of soothing self-talk, letting herself know it was fine to dip into her savings. That's what they were for she told herself—to give her just the right amount of freedom she needed to explore. She settled back in her seat and let out a long breath. Things were going to be fine. They were, *weren't they?*

Roxy drifted off to sleep at some point. She was awakened when the bus driver spotted a stop sign at the last minute and screeched to a halt. She blinked and looked out of the window. They were in New Orleans already? She was about to turn to the woman across the aisle and ask, but then she spotted a sign that said "*Craving Cajun?*" She couldn't *wait* to try the food. While her frame was petite, Roxy had a deceptively large appetite and enjoyed cuisine from around the world in rather large amounts.

That was one thing she could thank Ryan for—introducing her to international food. Along with

Mexican, Chinese, Italian, and Indian fare, they'd also adventured into less-explored culinary territory. They'd tried Indonesian, Jamaican, and Polish food, and they *loved* a good Ethiopian meal from time to time.

"Stop thinking about him," Roxy whispered to herself. "This is *your* new life—not his! Not yours to share, but yours *alone*." She was both extremely nervous and extremely exhilarated. She felt a buzzing sensation travel through her body. She couldn't wait to hop off the bus and locate the hotel where she was staying for the next month. *That* would be the beginning of her new life.

Roxy strolled down the New Orleans streets, pulling her case with one hand and holding Nefertiti's travel box in the other. She *sort of* knew where she was going, but she was enjoying the scenery and didn't mind too much that she was meandering a little. The sun was shining down, and Roxy felt sunny and optimistic.

She figured that she couldn't miss the guesthouse she was looking for. The pictures she'd seen made it look idyllic and so bright that she expected to squint. The flamingo pink frontage of the small hotel was what had attracted her, and when she found that they *did* accept pets, Roxy knew that it was the perfect place for her stay. The price was very reasonable, too, and they offered a hefty discount for month-long visits. Perfect.

Eventually though, Roxy stopped a sympathetic-looking woman in the street and asked her, "Do you know where Evangeline's guesthouse is?"

The woman's eyes flashed wide for a moment before she fixed her face into a smile. "Sure thing, sugar. You just go into the alleyway off this street, and it's a little way down there. You see it?" She pointed.

"Oh, sure, great," Roxy said.

The woman looked her over, her eyes curious. Roxy paused, wondering if she was violating any kind of local custom or unspoken rule. Perhaps her northern manners weren't up to snuff for those in the South. "Thank you, ma'am," she added, feeling a little uncomfortable but hoping she was saying the right thing.

"You're most welcome. Take care now."

Roxy followed the woman's directions and turned into a little alleyway. It was a very narrow cobblestone street, so narrow that only a small vehicle could have turned around in it. At the other end, there was an ivy-covered brick wall. Set within that was a tall, wrought iron gate beyond which she saw gravestones. Halfway down the alleyway, placed outside a café from which the most beautiful, sweet, pastry-baking smell was pouring, were set some tables and chairs. Her attention was quickly snatched away, however, by the building that faced them.

The sky above it was a deep, deep blue just as the website had promised, and Evangeline's was indeed where it was supposed to be, nestled among a huddle of old wooden buildings. The narrow three-story structure was pink as the photographs had shown, but that was where reality collided with Roxy's expectations. It was like a truck hitting a brick wall.

The pictures Roxy had seen must have been taken years and years ago. Now the paint was patchy—baby pink in some places, salmon in others, and almost white at the very top where it caught the most sun. Some of the wooden trim boards had black streaks running through them and were half rotted away. There was a little balcony on the third floor that looked like it would collapse at any minute, and while the windows were clean, one of them had a massive crack across it. Even the courtyard out front was a scrub of weeds. Roxy would have assumed it was abandoned if many of the windows hadn't been open.

Roxy gulped. What *on earth* had she done?

"Okay, Nefertiti. Here's home for the next

month." Roxy tried to sound cheerful, but she had a horrible sinking feeling. Her stomach was collapsing in on itself. Still, she thrust her head up and threw her shoulders back. There was no way she'd cry or break down or even doubt herself. She'd prove she wasn't boring. She'd prove she wasn't a pushover. She'd prove she wasn't afraid of anything. She'd prove she was adventurous, exciting Roxy, fully in control of her fabulous, fun, new life.

Roxy lugged her case over to the narrow weed-surrounded doorway and looked around for a doorbell. There wasn't one, so she knocked, plastering a smile on her face for whoever would greet her. She waited for something to happen. No one came, so she knocked again, more forcibly this time. The door opened with a long creak. Roxy peered inside.

In the hallway, she could see some rather grand-looking pieces of furniture, a large armchair, an armoire, and a huge mirror. They appeared to be antiques. An ornate wooden staircase with a worn carpet led upward and around a corner. On the wall, there was even a gilt-framed portrait of a young woman with blonde flowing hair wearing a hat and an old-fashioned, floral, frilly dress. There, though, the potential grandeur of the hallway ended.

The antique furniture was rendered incongruous next to a cheap-looking laminate front desk, and under a strip light that was far too bright to be comfortable, their shabbiness was laid bare. Gray cobwebby masses darkened the high white wooden ceiling, and Roxy spied a long-legged spider making its slow descent down the wall behind the unmanned desk. It was all very strange.

Just then, a woman walked across the hallway and toward the staircase. She didn't notice Roxy, who watched her closely. Her dark hair was piled up into a messy bun at the back of her head, and she wore a lime green jogging suit and bright white sneakers. Roxy estimated the woman to be in her mid-forties and might have guessed that she was an avid runner but for the little extra weight she carried around her middle and the full face of makeup she had on. Still slightly stunned by the situation, Roxy didn't gather herself to speak, even as the woman began to jog up the stairs.

"Meeeooowwww," said Nefertiti.

At the sound, the woman swung around and put one hand to her chest in shock, gasping and leaning forward before unfurling herself and laughing when she saw Roxy. "My goodness, you gave me a scare," she said. She came jogging back down the stairs.

"Sorry," Roxy said with a smile, glad for an opening to start a conversation. "This is Nefertiti. My cat. She can be quite vocal at times."

"I love cats," the woman said. "I used to have two. Not anymore, I'm afraid." She didn't elaborate.

"Oh, right," Roxy said. "So . . . are you . . . I'm . . . I'm meant to be staying here . . . I mean to say, I'm arriving."

The woman laughed at her but not unkindly. "They give a good welcome at this place, don't they?"

"Umm . . ." Roxy didn't quite know what to say. "So . . . you don't work here?"

"Oh, no," said the woman. "I'm a guest, too."

"Oh, right. Are you staying for Mardi Gras?"

The woman laughed again, but this time with a little bitterness. "For Mardi Gras and then some. I'm not quite sure what I'm doing next."

"Me either," said Roxy, her shoulders relaxing. "I have a month booked, with nowhere to go at the end of it."

The woman's eyes brightened perceptibly. "Well, then, we're in the same boat, aren't we?" She gave Roxy a conspiratorial grin. "Man trouble. Am I right?"

CHAPTER FIVE

"YOU ARE," ROXY said with a humorless chuckle before she could stop herself. She didn't normally share intimacies this quickly, if at all, but being alone in a new city seemed to have changed her.

The woman sighed dramatically. "Me too. I thought I had my life all figured out in New Jersey, but then my husband, well . . . let's say he found being faithful too taxing, and I found out about it. Stormed out that night with a suitcase, I did, and well, here I am!" She looked genuinely happy about it.

"Yeah, my boyfriend wasn't exactly Prince Charming either," Roxy said.

"Oh well, what man is really?" the woman said. "I'm Louise, by the way."

"I'm Roxy. Have you been here long?"

"About, um . . ." Louise looked up at the cobwebs on the ceiling, "three weeks now."

"How do you like it?"

Louise's blue eyes twinkled. "Well, it's not exactly a 5-star experience, and the cemetery at the end of the alleyway is a little off-putting after dark, but once you taste Evangeline's meals and the pastries from across the way, you'll *never* want to leave."

Now, *that* sounded good. Roxy had never been a big cook or baker while her boyfriend, wrapped in cotton wool by his mother as he had been, hadn't known how to do anything domestic nor had he been inclined to try. He'd have ordered takeout every day, but Roxy was too budget-conscious for that. They had eaten a lot of chicken stir-fry and baked potatoes. Good, wholesome food prepared by someone else sounded heavenly.

"And it has great bones."

Roxy frowned. "What does?"

"This place . . . good bones. I'm an interior designer," Louise explained. "And I'm just *desperate* to redecorate this place. My mind runs wild with how I could make it truly splendid. It's got great potential. It's a shame they want to tear it down."

"They do?" Roxy said. She wondered who "they" were.

"Yes," Louise said. "Why anyone would want to knock a building of such *heritage* down is beyond me. I'd tell them to . . ."

Nefertiti interrupted her with a very loud, very annoyed *meeeooowwww.*

"Oh!" Louise said. "That cat of yours is getting fed up with hearing us warble on. She wants to get settled in, I think."

Roxy was feeling apprehensive. Evangeline's looked like a dump. People wanted to tear it down, possibly before her month's stay was done, and who knew what horrors lurked in her room. She was torn between wanting to see more of the guesthouse and running back out the door. Was it going to be a cobweb-infested hovel? Or might it be quite charming in a rustic sort of way?

"Where *is* everyone?" Louise said, peering around. "Evangeline and Nat should be somewhere. Each one of them is crazier than the other, you know. And not exactly customer service whizzes either."

From the side door, in strode an androgynous young woman who looked to be in her early twenties. She was dressed head to toe in black: black T-shirt, black skinny jeans, black work boots. Her dark brown hair was cropped short, and her ears were adorned with multiple piercings. There was a tiny diamond stud in her nose. Her short-sleeved T-shirt revealed one entire arm covered in tattoos. Roxy, her eyes widening just a little, leaned in closer but quickly withdrew. She didn't want to be caught staring, especially not by this sharp-eyed, intimidating young woman.

"Well, what were you expecting at these prices?" the tattooed woman said with an English accent that was more Eliza Doolittle than Mary Poppins. "The Ritz?" A smirk pulled at her lips.

Louise chuckled, completely unembarrassed that her criticism of the guesthouse service had been overheard. "Oh, Nat. Not the Ritz. But maybe just a little common courtesy would be nice. I treat my house guests better, and they're not even paying."

"Of course you do," Nat said. "You don't get guests day-in and day-out though, do you?"

"Neither do you," Louise shot back, and there was a moment of stunned silence during which Roxy nervously looked back and forth between both women as she gauged the atmosphere. After a second, Nat burst out laughing, followed by Louise. Roxy joined in although not quite so uproariously. "This is Roxy and her cat, who seems to be getting restless," Louise said when she'd calmed down.

Nat nodded at Roxy. "Hi. I'm Nat. You're here for a month, aren't you?"

Roxy swallowed, wondering what she had gotten herself into. "That I am."

"Come on then, don't be shy. I'll haul your luggage up for you," Nat said. She grabbed the handle from Roxy and rolled the case to the stairs. "You've got the room at the top, the one with the balcony. You can't actually go *out* on the balcony, because it'll fall down if you do, but you can open the top of the doors. Sam, he's our handyman, sort of chopped them in half or something. Don't ask me how."

Roxy followed behind obediently, while Louise gave her a wide-eyed look and smile of sympathy. As they walked up the stairs, Roxy found there was no need for polite conversation, because Nat just kept talking and talking.

"Now, we don't have any AC up here, so you might roast like a chicken." When she saw Roxy chewing her lip, Nat laughed. "Nah, I'm just joking. Well, you might in July or August, but you're not with us that long. You just open the windows in the front and the back, and you'll get a breeze going through. No problem. I've stayed up here heaps of times. Breakfast is *en famille* and starts at 8, dinner is at 6."

"Okay," Roxy said. She followed Nat up the creaking staircase and took the opportunity to check out her tattoos. There were some roses and crosses and skulls, and a mishmash of bare-breasted women, unicorns, band names, and what looked like gargoyles or demons. There was a pirate ship in amongst the madness, too.

Nat caught her looking as they reached the third floor, and flashed her a grin. "I'm working out what to get next. I'm addicted." Then she opened the white wooden door to Roxy's room. There was a key in the lock. "Here you are," she said.

Roxy stepped into the attic room. It smelled a little of old wood, but also of freshly laundered cotton and delicious baked goods from across the narrow cobblestone alley. The half-door window contraptions didn't look as strange as they sounded and the windows were open wide, the white linen curtains flapping gently in the breeze.

The bed was large. A soft-looking white duvet lay over it. Across the room, next to an old armoire, there was a vintage dressing table with a white Louis-style stool. A rocking chair stood in the corner. The dark wooden floor was covered with a pale blue tasseled rug, and the whole place looked clean, welcoming, and comfortable.

Roxy sighed happily. She was pleasantly surprised.

"See? Not too shabby, huh? Like I said, dinner's at six, cocktails at five-thirty. See you then," Nat said. She unceremoniously plonked Roxy's case on the floor and spun around on her boot heel to leave her guest alone.

When Nat had left, Roxy sat down on the bed and looked around. She felt a thrill pulse through her. Nefertiti gave a tiny mewl from her carrier, and Roxy leaned down to let her out, cuddling the fluffy cat to her chest.

"This isn't too bad, is it, Nef? There's adventure ahead, possibilities. Anything could happen." She buried her nose in Nefertiti's soft, white fur, feeling the hairs tickle her nose. "And it's all going to be okay."

CHAPTER SIX

EVANGELINE SURPRISED ROXY in numerous ways, not least by the fact that she appeared to be at least eighty years old. The guesthouse owner was short, stocky, and with a tanned face creased a thousand times with wrinkles. In her ears were big gold hoop earrings and around her waist an apron lay over her blue dress patterned with tiny flowers.

She passed through the dining room from time to time, giving Roxy and Louise cheerful waves as they waited for their dinner. She had a spring in her step and twinkling green eyes lit up her face.

Every time she went through the white swinging door to the kitchen, a huge blast of fabulous-smelling air drifted outward—sausage and peppers and all kinds of savory flavors that Roxy couldn't quite put her finger on. Plus, something delicious was baking. Roxy sniffed the air and frowned, trying to identify the smell. *Oh,* it was *cornbread*!

"Smell awright, cher?" Evangeline said as she walked by, throwing Roxy a wink.

"Smells like *heaven,*" Roxy said cheerfully. She'd had a big tuna sandwich and a packet of chips on the bus on the way down but nothing since, despite the bakery across the road calling her name. Now she was ravenous. "I can't wait."

Evangeline looked her up and down as she pushed the swing door with her behind and grinned. "I think we need to get some good ole Creole spice into you, cher. Get you smiling and bright and a little round, like Louise here."

Louise laughed, pretending to be outraged. "Evangeline!"

Evangeline laughed. "Many men like a little more meat on the bones, Louise, don't 'cha know? If you've still got your eye on Sam . . ."

"I have not!" Louise protested, this time quite serious.

Evangeline snickered and disappeared into the kitchen, throwing another wink in Roxy's direction. She returned with two glasses. The drink inside was thick and creamy and white, with chocolate dust on top. "Your brandy milk punch. Usually for brunch, but since both of y'all missed that . . ."

"Thank you," Roxy said. "It looks scrumptious."

"It *is*," said Louise leaning in and whispering. "That's *why* I've been missing brunch. I've been putting on weight thanks to all this fabulous Creole cooking. I'm trying to get it off by running in the mornings and *not* sipping sugary drinks any time of day, but especially at breakfast. I can't keep my nose out of the sugar bowl if I start early. I'll be the size of a house before Evangeline's through with me if I'm not careful."

"Oh, life's too short to eat dull food, child," said Evangeline, overhearing as she once more made her way back into the kitchen. They heard her start to berate someone about something or other. Her words were laced with French and made Roxy pause as she sipped on her brandy milk punch, which was indeed scrumptious.

Roxy turned to Louise, "So how . . . ?"

She trailed off. It was clear Louise wasn't listening. She was flicking her hair behind her shoulder, sitting up straight, and pushing her lips into a pout. She was looking over Roxy's shoulder toward the doorway that led out from the lobby.

Roxy followed her gaze and despite Louise's bad manners, immediately appreciated what was causing her to behave in this odd fashion. The guy who had just come through the doorway was gorgeous.

He was tall for one thing and broad-shouldered for another, the kind of man who looked like he could lift small, slight Roxy with his little finger. The huge saxophone case he carried was dwarfed in his strong arms. He had tousled sandy hair and dark eyes that betrayed a little shyness but which were in direct contradiction to his confident walk.

"Hi Sam," Louise said. Her voice got a little high and childlike. Roxy suppressed a cringe.

Sam looked awkward. "Hi, Louise." He looked at Roxy, then back at Louise, obviously expecting an introduction, but Louise was far too busy batting her eyelashes at him to cotton on.

"I'm . . ." Roxy began, but unexpectedly, her voice caught in her throat. She cleared it and ended up in a coughing fit. She tried to sip a little punch to soothe her throat, but it didn't help. She grabbed a napkin, and Sam leaned his saxophone case against the wall to give her a firm pat on the back.

"Sorry," Roxy said through yet another cough, her voice tight and constricted. "I'm Roxy Reinhardt." Her eyes were watering, and she laughed at herself through the coughs—what else was there to do?

Sam opened his mouth, but before he could speak, a booming voice came from the doorway,

"And I'm Elijah Walder, if you don't mind!" An extremely slender man with sparkling eyes stepped in, holding aloft a white paper box like it was a tray. He came over to the table. He was wearing a black bow tie atop a white short-sleeved shirt printed with coffee cups. "Roxy, did I hear?" he said, sticking his free hand out.

"You did," Roxy said with a smile, taking his hand and shaking it quickly.

"Good to have another lovely, bright, and pretty flower around to liven up the place. Besides me, of course," he said. He strode away toward the kitchen door with his hips swaying from side to side as he did so; the box he held aloft moving in concert with them. "Better get these in to Evangeline," he said cheerfully, "before I get yelled at." He turned and cupped his hand to his mouth. "You know what she's like," he whispered.

Elijah was like a whirlwind, passing through the room so quickly no one had a chance to react. Roxy wasn't sure how she felt about being called a "lovely, bright, and pretty flower," but Elijah seemed to mean it kindly.

Sam thrust his hands into his pockets and laughed, watching the skinny man flounce into the kitchen. "Elijah owns the bakery across the street."

"He does?" Roxy asked. "It smelled *spectacu-*

larly good earlier. I'll be in there every single day, I'll bet."

Sam pulled up a chair from the next table. "I wouldn't blame you."

Louise leaned her elbows on the table and focused on him. From the way she was blinking owlishly in his direction, her mascara-thickened lashes batting furiously, Roxy doubted Louise had noticed Elijah at all. "Sam knows how to do *everything,*" Louise said, in a husky, low-toned voice.

"Is that so?" Roxy said.

"Of course not," Sam retorted.

"It *is,*" said Louise, leaning over and pushing Sam playfully on his bicep with her fingertips.

Sam blushed. Roxy reckoned it was with embarrassment but suspected that Louise would interpret it as a sign of attraction.

"He's got his own *very* successful laundry business," Louise continued. "He plays the sax like an absolute god. He fixes just about everything around here. *And* he manages to maintain an incredible physique." Her eyelashes flickered. "Did you bring that monster of a car with you today?"

Sam stared at the floor, then at the ceiling. He laughed. "Yes, yes, I did."

Louise turned to Roxy. "He has this *incredible* deep red car. What is it, Sam?"

"A Rolls Royce Phantom," he said. "But it's just . . . it's nothing. It's the one luxury I allow myself."

"It costs more than my *house!*" Louise said excitedly.

Sam turned quickly as they heard the front door open and close. A woman came into the room, and he sounded far too relieved when he said, "Sage! So good to see you!"

CHAPTER SEVEN

SAGE WAS A tall, willowy African-American woman. She looked to be in her late thirties. Long, mermaid-like hair in a mixture of pastel colors fell in ribbons to her waist. She wore billowing, purple linen robes. Around her neck were draped multiple chains, each one weighed down by a stone that lay on her breastbone. A laptop satchel sat at her right hip, the strap crossing her body. She raised her palms as she laughed good-naturedly at Sam's words. "It is a pleasure to lay eyes upon you, too, Samuel." The mellow tone of her voice was like honey and had that lovely New Orleans lilt. "Along with all the souls present here today," she looked at Louise and

Roxy, then around the room, "both seen and unseen."

"This is Sage Washington," Sam told Roxy. "She keeps the guesthouse website up to date and about a thousand other things." He flashed his eyes wide, and by the way he did so, Roxy could tell he meant a thousand other *unusual* things. But there wasn't a trace of mocking in his look; he treated Sage and the rest of them with great respect.

"The website?" Roxy said. Sage seemed such an ethereal soul, Roxy couldn't imagine her knowing what a computer was, let alone working one.

"Yes, sugar," Sage said. "But that's just my day job. I do tarot readings and all sorts of other spiritual work. I connect with the spirit world daily."

"*And* the not-so-spirit world," Sam said. They all laughed.

"It's true," Sage said. "I'd say connecting with the spirit world is my true calling, but I love my computer work, too."

Sage beamed a huge smile at Roxy, "So who are you, sugar?" she asked her.

"I'm Roxy. I'm from Ohio. I arrived here today."

"Greetings," Sage said. "You have a beautiful aura."

"Oh," said Roxy, a little taken aback. "Um, thank you."

"Evangeline not done yet?" Sage said, reaching

into her bag. "I could whip out my laptop and finish the last bit of programming for this client, before . . ."

"You won't be bringing any screens to *my* table!" Evangeline said, bursting through the kitchen door, carrying a steaming plate in each hand. "The only thing on this table is going to be my jambalaya. I made a special one for you, honey."

"I'm a vegetarian," Sage explained to Roxy. Elijah and Nat followed Evangeline out, all carrying plates.

"Put the tables together, why don't ya, Sam," Evangeline said.

"Sure," he replied, "but I've come for the washing. I heard you had a problem with the machine today."

"Yes, yes," Evangeline said impatiently. "You can pick it up later. Now, sit down and eat."

"Are you *sure* you don't want me to buy you a new washing machine? I could donate one of . . ."

"Charity," she hissed at him. "Now be quiet, we have a new guest."

"Sorry," Sam said. He looked a little shamefaced as he realized he'd been indiscreet. "Roxy, you'll love Evangeline's feast. Her food is the best."

Soon he'd dragged all the lace-covered tables into a neat row. Louise watched his bulging biceps the whole while, but the others arranged the chairs around the table as they anticipated tucking in to their hot plates of food.

Roxy noticed that Sam studiously avoided sitting next to Louise and ended up between Evangeline and Nat. The younger woman had bustled out of the kitchen and, with a grin, had plonked herself down gracelessly beside Roxy. Roxy couldn't tell what to make of the English woman. There was a definite edge to her, what with the piercings and the tattoos and the big biker boots, but she seemed nice enough. Elijah sat between Louise and Sage on the other side of the table.

"Now, Roxy," Evangeline said, "everyone else is used to this already, but let me tell you specially, cher. This is real Creole jambalaya, with salt pork, smoky sausage, shrimp, and a secret spice mix that's been in my family since before your grandmomma was born. It's got a little kick to it." She nodded at the jugs on the table—one of ice water, the other lemonade—and then at the bottles of red wine. "So go ahead and fill your glass with whatever beverage you'd prefer."

"That sounds like an invitation to me," Elijah said. He'd also joined them at the table. "Let's be getting ourselves going."

"But don't let Louise guzzle down all the wine over there," Evangeline said, "or she'll be flirtin' with the floor mop by the time the evenin's through."

"I will not!" Louise exclaimed.

Evangeline chuckled to herself. "If you say so, cher." Then she lifted her glass and said, "*Laissez les bons temps rouler!*"

Louise flashed Roxy a grin. "That's something about having a good time."

And they certainly *did* have a good time. The jambalaya was delicious, deep and rich with flavor and spice. The red wine was robust and warm, and it made Roxy feel all cozy. Best of all, Sam and Elijah got up after dinner and treated them to a live jazz show. Elijah demonstrated some deft finger work on the grand piano that sat in the corner, while Sam filled the whole room with beautiful, rich saxophone melodies. Soothed nearly to sleep, Roxy nibbled her dessert—a delicious pastry from Elijah's bakery—and felt the happiest and satisfied she had been in a long, long time.

Just as they were about to wrap up, Evangeline nodded at Sage, who reached into her bag and pulled out a well-worn deck of cards. Roxy wondered if she was about to start doing magic tricks, or if they were going to play poker. Neither was her sort of thing.

"Tarot cards," Louise explained to her. "It's their little after-dinner ritual." She rolled her eyes.

But no one was paying Louise much attention. Sipping on her wine, Evangeline watched keenly as Sage laid out the cards, face down.

"Let's go for a quick one today," Sage said. "I've got some programming to do before bed."

"I want a reading," Evangeline rushed to say. "About . . ." She widened her eyes significantly, "you know, this place." She looked over at Roxy and then back at Sage. "A fast one is fine."

"All right," Sage said. "Choose two cards."

Evangeline, her gnarled hand hovering over the cards, quickly pulled two back toward her. She flipped them over.

Sage gasped. "The Ten of Swords and The Tower. Oh gosh."

"What does it mean? What does it mean?" Evangeline asked.

Sage bit her lip. "Umm . . . well, it doesn't look good. But if we're looking for the positive . . ."

"I don't want the positive," Evangeline snapped. "I want the cold, hard truth."

Roxy peered over and saw that one of the cards depicted a man lying dead with ten swords sticking out of his back.

"Okay," Sage said. She gulped. "Well, the Ten of Swords means you're about to experience an unwelcome surprise. And . . ." She sounded reluctant to go on.

"And . . . ?" Evangeline said impatiently.

"Well, The Tower means everything's about to change—and not the rainbows and unicorns kind of change," said Sage.

"Hmm," Evangeline said. She was silent as she dipped her head and stared at the floor in deep thought, sipping her wine.

"Well, that's cheerful. Lucky they're just cards picked at random, eh?" Elijah said with a grin. He bit into his third pastry. Roxy wondered how on earth he stayed so slim, him being such a talented baker and surrounded by deliciousness all day. He was as thin and lanky as a beanpole.

Judging by the worn state of her card deck, Sage clearly believed heart and soul in tarot readings. She didn't say anything. She simply bit her lip and looked up at Evangeline. Her eyes were full of anxiety.

CHAPTER EIGHT

THE NEXT MORNING it took a while for Roxy to register where she was. Nefertiti was curled up in front of her face as usual, but she had to blink and lie back for a couple of seconds to remember that she was at Evangeline's guesthouse in New Orleans and that her regular life was indeed over.

It hadn't helped that she'd dreamed of Ryan giving her the most beautiful bouquet of flowers and telling her that she was his soul mate. Tears stung her eyes as she realized her dream hadn't been real. She'd have never called their love a grand passion, but when the relationship was working, it had been cozy and comforting and familiar, which was just how Roxy wanted life to be.

They'd had their problems, and Ryan was a real jerk at times, but she'd swept all that under the carpet to keep the relationship going. A fat lot of good that had done her. Now he was off, pursuing *his* Grand Passion it seemed, and Roxy was alone with no job, using up her precious savings without a plan. She stared at the ceiling. Was she really here because of a *commercial?* At the time, her decision had felt so *right*, like the universe had ordered stars in the perfect configuration just for her. Now it seemed ridiculous.

"Oh, Neffi, what have I done?" she said. Nefertiti pushed her nose under Roxy's chin and purred loudly as her owner tickled her. Roxy sighed. "Well, at least *you* sound happy."

She hauled herself up, wondering what she was going to do for the day, and the day after, and the day after that. She knew there was a Mardi Gras party in the area that night—Louise had told her—but Roxy was *not* in a party mood.

Even after a shower in the tiny bathroom and slipping into one of her favorite outfits, a denim sundress with a large ruffle neckline and lace hem, Roxy looked into the mirror and sighed heavily again. She tried a smile. It was little and pathetic, only just turning up the corners of her mouth, but it was a smile nonetheless. She inched her feet into silver sandals that sparkled with rhinestones and bent over to feed Nefertiti using the little carry bowl and one of the cat food sachets she'd brought along with her. Her cat tucked in with delight. Unlike her owner, she was unperturbed by her surroundings. "Maybe *I'll* feel better after breakfast," Roxy said.

But her image of beignets—a type of square donut that New Orleans is famous for—and coffee while reading pamphlets that would tell her about local tourist spots she should visit was shattered by the sound of raised voices in the hallway. She could hear them as she came down the stairs. She tried to make them out. One was easy. It was the quivering but fierce tones of Evangeline. The other was a man's voice, one she didn't recognize.

"I've told you 'no' a thousand times, haven't I? No, no, no, and no. When will you people get that message into your head, huh? Are you stupid or just senile?" Evangeline raged.

The man's voice was tense. "You and I know that you're pathetic and desperate clinging onto this dump of a place. Do what any right-thinking person would do and take the money."

"Like hell, I will!" Evangeline shot back.

They were so embroiled in hurling insults, they barely seemed to notice Roxy walking past. Evangeline was like a crackling, spitting fire. The man was losing his temper, too. His face was red, and he had a bead of sweat in his mustache. He was very tall and snappily dressed, but Evangeline didn't seem the least bit intimidated, even though he positively towered over her.

Roxy slunk into the dining room, her nerves on edge. She looked around the room to see pastel-haired Sage tapping away at her laptop, absent-mindedly eating a beignet, her eyes glued to the screen. She seemed to be completely oblivious to the drama unfolding in the hallway.

Louise was there too, sitting at a table in her running gear, her hair scraped back into a ponytail. She smiled at Roxy sheepishly and beckoned for her to come over and sit opposite. Roxy had planned to sit alone, but she wasn't sure how she could now, not without looking very rude.

"Morning," Louise said.

"Good morning," said Roxy, making an effort to sound cheerful.

"I'm . . ." Louise's eyes darted about awkwardly as she sipped her coffee. She looked down at her bowl of fruit. "I'm so embarrassed about yesterday." She lowered her voice. "I think I came on a little strong with Sam, don't you? You know, with the flirting?"

Roxy shifted in her seat, not knowing what to say. Louise stared at her with eager eyes. "Oh, I don't know," Roxy said eventually. "I'm most definitely *not* a relationship expert."

Louise puffed out a weary breath and leaned back in her chair. "Me either. I mean, he's good looking, and tall and talented, but I've just gotten out of a marriage, for goodness' sake. I think I just like him being around." She laughed self-consciously. "He's quite a comforting figure. Any time anything goes wrong around here, it's like, 'Oh, Sam'll fix it.'" She wiggled her head from side to side as she spoke.

Roxy nodded. "Talking of things going wrong . . ." She was about to ask what on earth was going on with Evangeline and the suited stranger outside in the hallway, but before she could, Evangeline herself stormed in and over to Sage's table. She dropped into the chair opposite and buried her head in her hands. Roxy was pretty sure she was crying.

Sage came out of her laptop daze. "The cards don't tell lies," she said. She rubbed Evangeline's arm.

"Maybe I should sell. That guy, Richard Lomas, certainly thinks so," Evangeline said. She pulled one hand away from her face and thumbed in the direction of the lobby where Roxy had passed her arguing with the man. The elderly woman roughly wiped her eyes with a napkin and sat up straight, jerking her arm away from Sage. "He works for TML Property Developers. He says it would be better for me to retire and put this place up for sale—specifically so he can buy it. Thing is, he's right. There are more repairs than I can keep up with and not enough guests. And the ones we have barely bring in enough money to take care of 'em. But he wants to tear the old girl down. Seems no one values New Orleans heritage no more. Y'all want to demolish these beautiful old places and build shiny, soulless apartment complexes in their place."

"Not everyone," Sage said. "Not you."

"Perhaps swimming against the tide is a waste of darn time, after all," Evangeline said bitterly. "Maybe I *am* standing in the way of *development* and *progress*. If I sold to Richard Lomas or some other developer, I could walk away and buy a nice little cottage. No more gettin' up at 6 AM to cook and clean for other people. I could sleep in and grow a pretty yard to sit in. I could get a little dog." She brightened up at the thought.

Nat came out of the kitchen, a white frilly apron over the top of her dark, edgy clothes. Her gaze flitted over Evangeline's face, and then to Sage. "Oh, what is it now?" she said, exasperated. "Can't be that you're bottling it, surely?" Nat said.

"I'm not sure I want to run a guesthouse no

more, cher," Evangeline replied, wearily. "Much as I love the people. And the cooking, now and again."

"So what are you going to do?" Nat said, deadly serious now. Her wide, amused eyes were filled with concern, and a small frown creased her forehead. "Chuck me out onto the street?" Her voice rose high with tension on the last word.

Louise called over. "*I'll* hire you when I buy one," she said to Nat. "I'd *love* to have a little guesthouse just like this."

"You try runnin' one 'fore you say that," Evangeline said. "Especially *this* one. What with the upkeep and the dry rot and everythin' wearin' out because it's all 100 years old, it's not easy. You have to have a real love of old architecture."

Roxy felt like she was in an alternate universe. She'd never been in a place where staff and guests spoke so freely to each other. It was almost like they were a bickering, but affectionate, family. Growing up, it had just been Roxy and her mom. There had been no extended family, and things had always been tense and difficult.

These easy exchanges, these expressions of feeling, the acceptance that the people around her showed for one another was unfamiliar to her, but she liked it. It felt refreshing. She felt a little like an outsider right now, but maybe, in the month she would be there, she'd learn to fit in, and this level of honesty and sense of freedom would rub off on her.

Louise ate her last piece of fruit. "Well, I'm going to have to think of *something* to do long term. I can't be a lady of leisure for the rest of my life. I'm too young for that even if I could afford it." She stood. "Anyhow, I'm off for my jog. Gotta run off last night's dinner." She stretched her arms above her head and gave them all a wave as she headed out.

"Now, what I *actually* came out here for was to ask you, Roxy," Nat said, "what you would like for breakfast? We have eggs, sausages, bacon, grits, biscuits, muffins, pancakes, omelets, toast . . ."

"Wow!" Roxy said. Talk about options! She would certainly be having fun with her breakfasts over the next month, but she was still set on her original vision. "Do you have beignets, too?"

"As long as I haven't eaten them all," Nat said, throwing her a wink. She leaned her head toward the kitchen. "Yep, yep, we do. Anything to drink?"

"Coffee, please. With cream and sugar."

"Coming right up."

"Now, Evangeline," said Sage as sternly as she could with that smooth-as-cream voice of hers. "I got up early to finish my programming job, so I have the day free. What can we do to cheer you up?"

"Me?" Evangeline said, incredulous. "I don't

need cheering up, cher." Her eyes belied her words but then sparkled with appreciation at the kindness Sage had shown her. She slapped her thighs. "I've got plenty of jobs to be gettin' on with." She pushed the three-quarter length sleeves of her green, floral print dress up over her elbows and headed to the kitchen. "You know, that Richard Lomas might not agree," she said, pointing to the place outside the room where she and the red-faced man had been arguing. "But I believe that this place is wonderful." She smiled at Roxy. "You have a good day, now, cher."

Sage watched Evangeline's retreating figure as it disappeared into the kitchen before turning to Roxy. "What are you doing today, sweetheart?" she asked. "I'm heading to our local botanica. That's a spiritual supplies store. It may not be your thing, but it's a great walk over there, and the sun is blessing us with its rays this morning. Nat's coming. What do you say?"

Roxy smiled. She felt quite comfortable with Sage despite her strange ideas. "Sure," she said. "I'd love to see more of the city. When do we leave?"

CHAPTER NINE

AS IT TURNED out, Roxy loved the botanica. She'd never been in such a place before. She breathed in its musky, sweet smell as she peered at all the unfamiliar objects on the shelves. There were little statues of Mother Mary, the saints, and other figures she didn't recognize. There were candles in every color, oils in tiny bottles, and so many scents, Roxy became intoxicated. There were crystals, engraved boxes, a basket of pewter "charms." There were even snowglobes labeled "Love," "Money," and "Revenge."

Nat stood in the doorway, her arms folded over her chest. She looked distinctly unimpressed. "Come *on,*" she kept saying. "How hard is it to choose between a bunch of candles or a handful of crystals?" Roxy looked up and saw pulses of anxiety play across Nat's face. She looked disturbed by the energy of the store though she did clutch a packet of incense sticks.

Sage smiled, her eyes appearing only half-focused. "I've ventured outside the realm of time so that I may deeply pleasure my soul."

"Yeah, I'm sure Evangeline will buy *that* when I tell her why I'm late," Nat grumbled.

Roxy had no idea what to buy. She turned another corner and came upon a whole new assortment of seemingly random objects—a huge collection of silk flowers, bottle after bottle of Florida Water, silver goblets filled with shiny black stones, and a line of human skulls which looked much too real for Roxy's liking. She took the time to remind herself that, of course, they *weren't* real. They couldn't possibly be. But still . . .

She could have stayed to explore the store all day until she came upon the skulls. They sent a jolting shiver up her spine, and she went to join Nat at the entrance. By now, Nat was mumbling "weirdos" and "absolute rubbish" under her breath. Feeling a little intimidated by this rather brittle, young English woman, Roxy pretended to study a rack of herbs while they waited for Sage to finish up.

On the way back to the guesthouse, Sage and

Nat had a good-natured—but still heated—argument. Nat started it.

"So Sage, what miracle in a bag did you buy this time?"

"Candles for my archangel altar," Sage said, ignoring Nat's sarcasm.

"And what's *that* when it's at home?" Nat asked with a snort.

Roxy, too, was a little curious and equally skeptical, but she would never have been so outwardly scornful.

"An archangel altar is a portal to facilitate contact with certain benevolent spirits from the unseen world," Sage said serenely.

"Oh brother," Nat said, rolling her eyes.

"No one's asking *you* to believe in it, honey," Sage said smoothly. "It's not your fault. Society has conditioned us to not believe anything beyond the bounds of modern science. And that's okay."

Nat shrugged. "Meh. I didn't like science at school either. I like things I can see and touch, and you can't see atoms, can you? Well, they can with their super-super-super-microscope thingies, but not with 'the naked eye.' No, I like to think about what I can see right in front of me. Like now, we have to get back to Evangeline's because I have to make lunch, and if I don't, she's going to go crazy on me. That's what *I* believe in."

Sage sighed. "Well, everyone's different."

Nat looked her up and down. "And thank goddess for that!"

Roxy hated the mounting tension, but then Nat and Sage burst out laughing, and Nat threw her arm around Sage's shoulders. "I do love you, you crazy witch lady."

Sage chuckled. "And I love you, too, you . . . you . . . thug!" They all laughed at that.

"Oh, look, is that Sam?" Roxy said, pointing a little way down a side street on the other side of the road. His flashy car was parked on the sidewalk. Sam was wearing reflective sunglasses and looked pretty flashy himself. He was speaking with a couple of guys who looked a little shady. They saw Sam count out a wad of bills and hand them to one of the men. Roxy frowned. "What is he doing?"

Nat shrugged her shoulders. "Who knows? He's very private about what he does outside of the guesthouse and laundry."

Roxy continued to look over as they passed and wondered what he could be doing. The transaction didn't look very savory.

When they reached the narrow cobbled street that housed Evangeline's guesthouse and Elijah's wonderful bakery, they spotted a woman wearing a navy pencil skirt and jacket up ahead of them. It was hard *not* to spot her because just then she caught the heel of her bright red stiletto in the cobblestones and went flying forward. She collapsed onto one of Elijah's tables and stayed there prostrate over it for a few seconds until she peered around to see who might have seen her ungainly fall. Carefully, she straightened up, tugged on her skirt, and wriggled it back into place. She smoothed down her thick, shoulder-length blonde hair, flicking what might have been crumbs off her jacket.

As Roxy, Sage, and Nat got closer, they could see the woman was furious. A deep frown creased her forehead, and she blew air from her nose like an angry bull. Tears shone in her eyes too, and when she noticed the women, she flushed a deep shade of pink. "Oh . . ." she said. Roxy felt a little sorry for her.

"Hi there," Nat said, uncharacteristically smiley. "Have you come to stay at Evangeline's?"

"Evange—? *That!*" the woman replied. She spun around, looking up at Roxy's rickety balcony in disgust. Roxy began to feel distinctly *less* sorry for her. "Of course not. I'm looking for Richard Lomas. Have you seen him?" Her eyes like lasers drilled into the three of them, and her lips, bearing remnants of red lipstick that matched her shoes, curled into a snarl.

Nat crumpled her brow.

"The name sounds familiar," Sage said. "Um . . ."

"Tall guy," the woman said, flicking up her chin. "Snappy suit. Property developer. Attitude to match."

"Oh!" everyone said, even Roxy.

"Yes, we know him." Nat crossed her arms over her chest. "Are you one of them? The demon developers?"

"No," the woman practically spat. "My name is Mara Lomas. He's my husband. How do you know him?"

"He's been trying to persuade Evangeline to sell her building to him. So he can tear it down," Nat said. "But it's not for sale."

Roxy wasn't at all sure Nat should be sharing this kind of information with a stranger on the street, but before she could say anything, Mara started snarling again.

"Well, if you see the slippery snake, tell him I'm in town, I know exactly what he's done, I know all about his *cozy* little double life *and* his mistress." She laughed bitterly. "And tell him, he'd better say goodbye to his beloved Aston Martin too, because that's the *first* thing I'm going to make my lawyers take from him." She looked the three of them up and down. No one knew quite what to say. She nodded her head fractionally upward. "Just tell him I'm looking for him, okay?"

Nat shrugged. "Okay."

"Good." Mara began to stride away purposefully, but her exit wasn't quite as dramatic and impressive as it could have been. She had to quickly change her stride to a totter as she picked her way carefully over the cobblestones in her three-inch heels.

"I hope for blessings on your soul," Sage called out after her. She looked genuinely concerned.

Mara waved dismissively. "Pray for *his* soul," she called back. "He's going to need all the protection he can get!" Her voice reverberated around the small side street; then she turned the corner and was gone.

CHAPTER TEN

"WHOA," WHISPERED ROXY. She wished *she* had been a little more Mara-esque toward *her* ex. Some threats and stiletto strutting might have been quite empowering, but at least she hadn't sobbed down the phone or had some other humiliating reaction. She had retained her self-respect.

Roxy's shoulders slumped when she thought of her ex-boyfriend. Without any idea of who his new girlfriend was or what she looked like, Roxy tortured herself with images of a tall, picture-perfect bronzed beauty with a gorgeous curvy body and thick, flowing, long hair. She'd be a brunette, of course, Roxy was sure. Ryan had loved to remind Roxy that he preferred dark-haired women. Dark-haired, *long-haired* women. As she considered this, she wondered whether she had been with someone who was deliberately cruel, who determinedly sought to undermine her, who *wanted* her to feel bad about herself? A frown creased the bridge of her nose.

"Are you all right?" Sage said. The African-American woman peered at her with concern.

"Oh, yes, yes, I'm fine." Roxy woke up from her daydream and shook her head. "Yes, fine. Um, I must go. I'd better feed Nefertiti."

"You can let her roam around, you know," Nat said. "We just have to make sure the front door is closed for a bit so she doesn't go outside and get lost. To make sure, Evangeline will put butter on her paws for a couple of days. Then she'll *never* stray far."

Roxy smiled. "Sounds like a plan."

"Aha!" a voice from behind them called out.

They turned to see Elijah coming from his bakery, holding his signature white boxes. "You've got a beignet monster staying with you, huh?" he said. "Evangeline's alone would keep my bakery going at the moment. Is it you, Roxy?" He narrowed his eyes as he pointed a finger and wagged it accusingly.

"Look at how skinny she is," Nat said, laughing. "She's not scarfing down thousands of those things now, is she?"

Elijah gestured down at his own impossibly wiry body.

"Not everyone has the metabolism of a stick insect," Nat said.

He gave her a fake frown and waggled his finger again. "You'll never get a job anywhere else, Miss, talking to people like that. I hope you're kissing Evangeline's shoes."

Nat laughed again, but a little less heartily this time. She punched him in the arm.

"Anyhow," Elijah said, "who's coming to see the Krewe du Vieux with me tonight? Their parade is in the French Quarter. I was thinking of heading there then maybe taking a cruise down the river."

"Wow!" Roxy said, her eyes lighting up. "I'll come!" She paused. "What's the Krewe du Vieux?" she added.

"It's a Mardi Gras parade known for its wild, adult themes. They usually include political comedy, and they have some of the best brass and traditional jazz bands in New Orleans," Elijah said.

"Sounds great!" Roxy replied.

"If we're feeling brave enough we'll hit their after-party, too. It's called the Krewe du Vieux Doo. Try saying *that* fast," he added.

"Krewe du Vieux Doo, Krewe du Vieux Doo, Krewe du Vieux Doo, Krewe du Vieux Doo, Krewe du Vieux Doo, Krewe du Vieux Doo," Nat said.

"Okay, okay," Elijah retorted, flapping his free hand to calm her down. "I didn't mean for you to take me literally."

"Krewe du Vieux Doo," Sage said, elongating the vowels in the words, and shaking her head. "They should respect the vast spiritual heritage of Voodoo more carefully if you ask me. They're making a mockery of it. You know, it's a tradition thousands of years old from Central and West Africa."

"Yeah, yeah," Nat said. "But they just want to have *fun!* Relax a bit, Sage. You can't take *everything* seriously. Elijah, I'll be there. With Roxy *and* Sage."

"Sounds more and more like a party every moment," Elijah said with a grin. "I like it. Sam's coming, too."

"That means Louise will be there with her eyelashes," said Nat. "Oh, bless her little heart."

That evening, they all met in the lobby and walked down to the French Quarter together. Sage was in her trademark flowing robes, a pale lilac this time. The color matched the tones in her hair. Nat also wore what was proving to be her uniform—black jeans and a scary-looking band T-shirt. A big pink tongue splayed out from a skull and crossbones that was emblazoned across the front of her top. In contrast, Louise wore a figure-hugging baby blue dress and stood too close to Sam, who kept edging away. He was more conventional in jeans and a button-down shirt. To Roxy's eye, and probably Louise's, he looked more handsome than ever. Roxy had kept things simple with a long patterned rust-colored skirt and a cream peasant top, but Elijah wore a bright purple suit with a pair of shiny black crocodile shoes.

Evangeline stood at the doorway, Nefertiti in her arms. The guesthouse owner had indeed given the cat butter that afternoon, and Nefertiti had appreciated the treat enormously. The elderly woman watched the younger people with tears welling up in her eyes. "This is the last time you'll do this, leave from here to go to the parade. It's the end of an era," she said. She snuggled her head against Nefertiti's.

"You've decided to sell?" Sage asked.

Evangeline nodded. "I've called that developer. It's all over. This place will be just rubble by the en' of the summer." Her voice caught in her throat. "So y'all go on. Jump up in the carnival for me, and send ole Evangeline's out with the best of memories, won't ya?"

"Of course we will," Louise said. She wrapped Evangeline in a hug.

They walked to the French Quarter a little subdued, but Elijah kept telling everyone jokes and striding forward cheerfully. He made everyone feel a little better. Everyone, that is, except Nat. She kept looking up and around at all the buildings and didn't join in with any of the conversations.

Roxy watched her for a while. She wondered what was causing Nat to be so nervous and if she knew her well enough to ask her if she was all right. After a few minutes' observation, Roxy decided against it. She didn't want her head bitten off for reaching out, and experience had taught her that might well happen. Instead, she fell into step beside Nat and they walked side by side in silence.

New Orleans looked truly beautiful as they walked through it. There were string lights dotted around the tops of buildings and hanging over roadways. They were like little fairies who had decided to bless the city with their magic. It was warm for the time of year, too.

"Lovely, isn't it, this place?" Roxy said to Nat.

"Not really," Nat replied. "I've seen better." She sounded nonchalant and dismissive, but her voice cracked.

Silence fell once more. They walked on for a while, falling behind the others. "So how did you end up here?" Roxy tried again.

"No particular reason."

"But you must have come here for something. You don't end up in New Orleans by accident." Roxy was surprising herself. She wasn't usually so forward.

"It's a long story," Nat said, staring resolutely ahead. She quickened her pace and walked away as Roxy wondered what that long story might be.

CHAPTER ELEVEN

APART FROM WHAT Elijah had told her, Roxy had no idea what to expect from the Krewe du Vieux parade, but she was very excited and curious to see it. They had gotten there early, and yet the streets were already lined with people waiting for the parade to start. The atmosphere on the street was buzzing as the group settled down at a table outside a fancy-looking restaurant where the tables were covered in linens and a replica oil lamp sat on every one. The air was getting a little colder. The sun had set and the cool wind rushed over the darkened Mississippi River.

"Café Brûlots all round to warm us up?" Elijah asked.

"Oh, yes!" everyone except Roxy said. She had no idea what a Café Brûlot was.

Sam sat down beside her. "You're in for a real treat," he said. "Café Brûlots are spiced liqueur coffees that they flame up right in front of you, watch."

Roxy looked at him warily. He seemed like such a good, generous person, but she wondered whether he was completely honest. There was that business with giving money to men on the side street and the flashy car. How did he afford such a thing? Was she just being paranoid? Oh, why was life so confusing?

A waiter in a jacket and bow tie came up to the table rolling a cart with a bowl set on top. He straightened and poured some liquor into a ladle.

"That's cognac and curaçao. The spices are already in the bowl," Sam said in his lovely low voice. Roxy could feel the heat of his body next to her, and she struggled to keep her heart from racing. After all, he was extremely handsome. And Louise was right. He emanated stability and capability. He seemed like a guy who would step in and save the day if necessary, whatever it took. Safe. Solid. A protector. Still, she couldn't put her worries to rest.

The waiter set the alcohol on fire, and blue flames leaped up in a chaotic fiery dance. He ladled the flaming liquid over an orange that had been mostly peeled, its skin trailing downward in a spiral into the bowl. More blue flames jumped up, but the waiter doused them with a brown liquid.

"And there's the coffee going in!" Louise said. She giggled girlishly and brushed her hand against Sam's.

He jerked his away with a laugh. "Indeed, and now for the sugar." He got up and went to stand next to Elijah.

The waiter poured sugar into the bowl and ladled the spiced coffee, cognac and curaçao mixture into small coffee glasses. He finished by adding a dollop of whipped cream. "Voilà!"

The table burst into applause.

"Bravo, bravo!" Elijah said, and he gathered up the coffee cups as best he could, carrying three between his fingers.

Sam scooped up the other three coffees, and soon they were all sipping and sighing with delight. Roxy savored hers, drinking it ever so slowly. The brandy and coffee and cream together were warming, but the hints of orange and spice and cinnamon took the drink to a whole new level of "ahhhh."

"Like drinking a hug," Nat said.

Roxy smiled. "It *is* kind of like that!" She winced a little at the strength of the brandy, though. "They don't scrimp on the alcohol, do they?"

Sam laughed. "They certainly don't."

Just then, police sirens started to blare, and blue lights flashed among the crowd.

"Hey, what's going on?" Roxy said, getting up and looking around. She was a little jumpy at the best of times—the result of growing up with a mother who could be unpredictable. Sirens made her edgy.

"They're clearing the road for the parade!" Sage said, clapping her hands. "Let's go stand a little nearer and get a good look!"

The crowd wasn't dense, and they managed to get a great spot almost immediately. Roxy's head swirled a little when she got up, though. The brandy had been strong, and she was beginning to regret not having eaten anything since breakfast.

Brightly dressed people, some adorned with strings of fairy lights, began to walk down the middle of the street while music pumped away in the background. Roxy smiled at the colorful spectacle, the cold air hitting her face, joyous people all around her. She saw a woman with blue hair, in a pink cone hat, a purple basque, and fishnets. She waved extravagantly to the crowd. Her friend, wearing a pirate hat, skull mask, and a ruffled gown, swayed silently to the music.

"Look at the horse!" Sage said, nudging Roxy.

Roxy peered down to the end of the street and saw a large, stocky, dark brown horse making its slow way toward them. It was pulling a parade float dressed in lights and swathes of bright fabric. A huge jester's head was displayed on the front of the float while a couple of people stood on top of it wildly waving colored rags around a sculpture of the Statue of Liberty.

Next came a large group of people dressed in old-time clothes—men with tailcoats and tricorn hats, ladies with powdered faces, towering curly wigs, and corseted dresses in all kinds of vivid colors: fuchsia, turquoise, crimson, and canary yellow. They all laughed and joked and danced and drank as they proceeded down the center of the street.

Roxy couldn't help but bounce along to the rhythm of the music. Most everyone did, and Elijah was near leaping about. Only Nat stood still, looking uncharacteristically shy and withdrawn. Roxy thought she might try to talk to her again later, but for now, she was entranced by the throbbing beat, happy screams, whoops, and cheers that reverberated all around her.

Soon a brass band was marching by, a whole assortment of men and women playing French horns and trumpets and saxophones and other instruments that Roxy didn't know the names of. A percussion section followed behind with a man banging a big bass drum. The music was happy and cheerful and somewhat disorderly. It made Roxy want to dance.

As soon as the parade had passed and people milled around, Elijah jumped out into the road with them. "Who's hitting the after-party with me?"

"I'd much prefer the boat ride," Sage said.

"I think I need to eat something," said Roxy. "That Café Brûlot has gone straight to my head!"

"Me too," Louise said, giggling. She stumbled into Sam and put her hand on his chest. "Oops! Silly me!"

Sam carefully moved her hand away and steadied her on her feet. "Whoa there, lady," he said.

"What about you, Nat?" Elijah said, looking over. She had her arms crossed protectively over her chest, and her face was solemn. "Cat got your tongue this evening?"

All of a sudden, Nat burst into tears, shocking everyone. She quickly swallowed and wiped her eyes hurriedly, saying, "Sorry, I'm sorry." She turned to leave. The group followed her.

"What's wrong, cher?" Elijah said, putting his arm around her like a big brother.

"I've been beside myself all evening. What *am* I going to do? Evangeline's closing!" Nat said, her voice strangled by another suppressed sob. "I won't be able to stay!"

"What do you mean?" Sage said. "You can get another job."

"But that's just it!" said Nat. "I can't." She lowered her voice. "I don't have a work visa. I came to the US to work as a nanny. Of course, that all went to pot, as does *everything* in my life, but Evangeline took me on and paid me under the table. It was lovely of her, and I'll be eternally grateful . . . but . . . but, basically, I'm . . . well, I'm not legal!"

"Oh," Elijah said, taken aback. Sage leaned over and, encircling Nat's shoulders with her arm, kissed her on the head. "There, there."

Louise smiled brightly. "Well, you don't have to worry, sweetie. I've made up my mind. I'm not going to let Evangeline sell the place to a developer just so he can tear it down. I'm going to buy it myself. I intend to do it up and make it into an upscale boutique hotel. You can keep working there." Louise looked Nat over. "Maybe more . . . behind the scenes, but you'll get paid. We'll be one big happy family. Perhaps Evangeline will stay on and continue cooking. I sure hope so. I'm going to make her an offer she can't refuse as soon as I get back."

Sam said, "Louise, I was thinking of buying it, too." He looked uncomfortable. "I have some . . . uh . . . spare change lying around. It makes sense for Evangeline to sell especially to someone who will protect the building, but the thing is, I don't think she will hear of it. I've already floated the idea, and she says that I'm just interested in buying it as a favor for her. Her pride won't allow it! I think she's made up her mind to sell to this developer now. She'll get a decent price without sacrificing her dignity. Don't be surprised if she turns you down."

"That woman can be so stubborn!" Nat said.

"Indeed, she can," said Sage smoothly. "But everything will turn out all right in the end. The spirits will make sure of it."

"But what if they don't?" said Nat. "What if I end up being carted back to England? The whole point of leaving there was to start a new life. I have nothing to go back to."

Nat's words got Roxy thinking about her own situation. Where would she go once this month was up? What would she do? If this developer shut Evangeline's down right away, would she even be able to stay for the full month she'd booked? Would she get her money back? Roxy bit her lip, beginning to feel as bad as Nat did. Her own future looked just as uncertain.

CHAPTER TWELVE

"LET'S TALK ABOUT this tomorrow," Elijah said. "Come on, let's eat and drink all our troubles away tonight. Problems can wait until the morning."

He led them to a run-down restaurant with pool tables in the back. From the outside it was shabby. The paint peeled and a wooden door badly needed staining. Inside it was gloomy, but Roxy could see if she peered hard enough that the interior was . . . exactly the same as the exterior. The wooden tables and chairs had seen better days, and the tiled floor was cracked and uneven.

"Hello, André!" Elijah said loudly as he crossed the threshold. Everyone in the restaurant turned to look at him. "He owns this place," Elijah explained to the others.

André, the heavyset owner with a huge handlebar mustache said, "Elijah!" just as animatedly. He came over and embraced Elijah with a hug, slapping him on the back.

"Table for a million, please," Elijah said, gesturing at the group. He scanned his eyes over them all. "I mean, six."

Despite the surroundings that hadn't promised much, they had the most gorgeous meal. Roxy chose a chicken and andouille gumbo to start, a lovely thick, buttery, tomatoey, highly seasoned stew. Next, she had a shrimp étoufée, a dish chock full of shrimp on a bed of rice. It had a deep, spicy, but slightly sweet flavor that she just couldn't get enough of.

While they ate, they chattered away, even Nat, who seemed better for having gotten her worries out. Fueling their conversation was a crisp chardonnay that Elijah described as having 'undertones of oak and smoke.' Glass after glass had gone down easily. Despite having filled herself up with savory courses, and sharing a plate of pralines with Nat, Roxy felt quite light-headed when she stood up. Everyone else seemed pretty merry, too. All except for Sage, who was a teetotaler.

"Boat ride next?" Elijah said to everyone, his voice slurring a little.

"I think . . . I think I might just fall in the Mississippi River," Louise said. "Which one of you strong men will jump in and save me, huh?" She looked straight at Sam.

"Oh, will you stop making a spectacle of yourself?" Nat said, a little too loudly. Nat's inhibitions were quite low *without* any alcohol in her system, so after a few drinks, Roxy was pretty sure she would say anything she darn well pleased. Nat was about to prove her theory correct.

"Look at you. He's young enough to be your *son.* We all know you're going through some kind of midlife crisis, but please, find someone your own age."

Ouch. There was a horrible pregnant pause, and Roxy hoped this wasn't going to turn into an awful argument. Everyone watched Louise, waiting to see how she'd react.

She burst out laughing. "Oh, let me have my little fun. Ever heard of living it up?" She held out her empty glass. "Elijah, pour me some more!"

"I think you've had quite enough!" he said. "And I've had far too much to be some lifeguard if you fall out of the boat. Let's get you home."

Louise giggled. "Okay! Home time!"

While Elijah escorted a very wobbly Louise back to Evangeline's, Nat, Sage, Roxy, and Sam headed off to catch the boat. Roxy was relieved to get out of the hot restaurant. The thick, fragrant air had steamed up all the windows, and the chatter and laughter of the patrons, along with all the glass clinking and plate clattering, made the atmosphere loud and overwhelming. As she walked outside, Roxy enjoyed the cold air hitting her face once more, and the four of them meandered down to the riverfront.

Roxy couldn't help but notice Sam in the warm glow of the streetlights. She looked up at him. From her viewpoint, the backdrop was a dark sky, with a sprinkling of stars shining here and there. He caught her looking and smiled down at her.

Snap out of it, Rox! She shook her head and turned around. She saw some stragglers from the last of the parade.

"I can't see any boats," Nat said. She was a few steps ahead of them and a little unsteady on her feet. "I'll go check at the kiosk."

"I'm coming with you," said Sage. She linked her arm firmly in Nat's before she could wriggle away, and they made off into the night. Sam continued after them.

Roxy was watching the last of the parade performers. "Shoot, I should have gotten a photo!" she said. She pulled her phone out of her bag and lined up a shot before the performers disappeared from view. "Oh, it doesn't look that good," she muttered to herself and fiddled with her phone. "It's a little dark. Maybe if I turn on the flash?"

She got a couple of shots in but they weren't great either. She tried the zoom; it made everything blur. She decided to get a little closer.

Roxy was so intent on what she was doing she didn't notice she was alone at the riverside. As she walked forward, she sensed a tall, broad figure move up behind her. Momentarily, she thought it was Sam, until . . .

"Listen," a voice said behind her. "Give me that phone, or you'll regret it."

She spun around. "What?" before recoiling in horror.

There, in front of her was a man in a black and silver carnival mask, ribbons trailing from it. She gave a little scream. She looked over her shoulder, but the carnival stragglers had gone. So had her friends.

"You heard me," the man with the mask said. "Pay attention, I've got a gun." He patted his waist and moved closer. "You're a pretty little thing, aren't you?"

"Here, take it! Have the phone!" Roxy said, holding it out to him, her heart beating so fast she felt it would jump out of her chest. She began to back away. She fumbled her phone, and it fell to the ground.

The man walked up to her slowly, seeming to savor her fear.

"Sam!" she hollered. "Sam, help!"

"Sam, help!" the man mocked her. He pushed his face close to hers.

"Hey!" a voice bellowed through the still night air.

Sam had heard her. He came running. "Get out of here right now!" he yelled as he quickly covered the ground between them.

"Or what?" the man spat. He turned to face Sam.

"He's got a weapon!" Roxy shouted.

But Sam stepped right up to the man, his eyes filled with rage, his hands ready for a fight as he cleared the assailant by several inches. "I said get out of here," he said, in a quiet, intimidating voice. "Trust me, you're gonna want to do as I say."

The man jerked toward him, his face inches from Sam's. Sam didn't even flinch. Then, like an animal who knows that retreat is the better course of action in the face of a stronger foe, the man sloped away. Sam and Roxy stood frozen until he'd turned a corner and was out of sight.

"Oh my," Roxy said, dropping her hands to her sides and allowing herself to finally breathe.

"Are you all right?" Sam asked. He came closer, and put his arm around her shoulder, looking her over with concern in his eyes. "Did he hurt you?"

"No, no, not at all," Roxy said. "He just gave me a scare, is all."

"I'm so sorry that happened to you. On your first night out in New Orleans, too. That's bad luck. You must think we're all criminals now."

"No," said Roxy. "No, I don't. Not at all."

"Do you want to go back to Evangeline's?" he asked. "I'll walk you there if you want." Seeing her phone still on the ground, Sam picked it up and handed it to her.

Roxy took the phone from him. She thought about Sam's question. "No, I'd like to go on the boat ride, please."

Sam smiled. "You're a brave one, aren't you?"

"Not usually," Roxy replied.

"I don't believe you," he said.

Little did he know. They walked down the riverside together.

"So are you sure you like it here?" he asked after a while.

"It's only been a day, but so far I love it," Roxy said quietly. "I love the food, the atmosphere, the carnival, Evangeline's—everything! There's danger everywhere, I know that much."

Roxy had grown up in a tough neighborhood.

This wasn't the first time she'd been mugged. It was almost a daily occurrence where she came from. People who knew her were often surprised by how little these sorts of things rattled her. It was emotional situations that made her nervous.

"Good," Sam said. He paused before resuming, "What about . . . what about . . . the people?"

Roxy looked up. He looked away, and then looked back again.

She smiled and said softly, "The people are wonderful."

Just at that moment, they heard Nat's voice shouting back at them, cutting through the darkness. "There's one more boat tonight! It gets here in fifteen minutes!"

"Well, fifteen minutes isn't too long to wait," Roxy said.

"No," Sam agreed, with a half-smile Roxy found very attractive. "Not when there's good company to be had."

CHAPTER THIRTEEN

NEXT MORNING, THE atmosphere at breakfast was dire. Roxy was silent. Louise was sullen. Nat's service was fitful and slow. No one spoke. The fun of the carnival had passed. Only dejection and sore heads were left in its wake. Nefertiti had come downstairs with Roxy, but after a couple of minutes, she left. Plainly not even her cat could tolerate the mood and Roxy felt depressed. It felt as though she were living beneath a large dark cloud, one that could burst at any moment.

"Sam was right," Louise said to Roxy, eventually. "Evangeline rejected my offer. Said she was already committed to Lomas. She's expecting him here any minute to sign papers." A crash from the kitchen made both of them wince. It was followed by raised voices and finally a heavy silence.

Roxy pondered this news. If Evangeline sold the guesthouse, where would she go? She couldn't imagine staying in any other establishment. Roxy then berated herself for getting attached so quickly. She barely knew these people. So why then, did she want to go magic shopping with Sage again, and learn more about those mysterious tarot cards? Why then, did she want to cut through Nat's tough exterior and become friends? Why then, did she want to keep eating Evangeline's exquisite meals and learn about New Orleans culture? And why then, did she want to stick around and get to know Sam?

Roxy munched through her beignets. She couldn't even touch her coffee—it reminded her too much of the Café Brûlot from the previous night, which now lived on as a lingering headache.

Once she was done eating, Roxy sat alone at the table, flicking through the local newspaper aimlessly. There was coverage of the carnival procession alongside the usual articles about properties for sale and local events. They made Roxy feel a little lost and lonely. Much as she liked it, New Orleans wasn't home, but Ohio wasn't either. Nor was with her mother. She didn't *have* a home. The only constant she had in her life was Nefertiti. Everything felt bleak, despite the beautiful morning sunlight streaming through the windows.

"We were supposed to sign the papers this morning, and now he doesn't even have the decency to show up!" Evangeline shouted in the kitchen.

Roxy heard the clatter of a saucepan. "I've had enough!" Nat shouted back. "If you're so desperate to sell this place and ruin everything, I'll get him for you myself! What hotel is he staying at?"

"I don't have a choice, Nat!"

"What hotel is he staying at?" Nat repeated fiercely.

"The gosh-darned Fontainebleau!" Evangeline shot back at her.

"Right, then!" Nat stormed out of the kitchen and threw her apron down on the table next to Roxy.

Despite Nat's fury and complete unwillingness to hide it, Roxy wasn't so intimidated by her anymore. If anything, she felt quite comfortable. After all, they were in the same boat. If Evangeline's closed down, both of them would have a serious problem.

"I'm coming with you," Roxy said, surprising herself with her boldness.

"Fine," said Nat. She was already striding out of the room, her chin stuck up high. Roxy had to scurry behind her to catch up, even when they were out on the street. Nat had long legs and kept up quite a pace in her heavy combat boots. They marched to the hotel in complete silence.

The hotel lobby was a shiny, marble affair, and Nat couldn't have looked more out of place. She didn't seem to care, though, or even notice. She marched right up to the front desk.

"I want to speak to a guest, Richard Lomas, please. Can you ring his room?"

"Of course . . . er, Miss," the young man at the desk said, looking taken aback. He looked Lomas up on his computer and dialed a number on the phone. "I'm afraid there's no answer."

"Try again, please," Nat said firmly.

"We have a policy—"

"Fine," said Nat. "Can you go up and see if he's there?" She paused, her eyebrows arched. "Please."

The man clenched his jaw as he stood up. "Yes, Miss," he said insincerely. "And who should I say wants to see him?" He looked her up and down. Nat's tattoos stood out even more than normal in the staid, chrome and neutral-shaded lobby.

Nat straightened up and held her head high. "The management of Evangeline's. He'll know."

"Please wait over there," the man said. He gestured toward a couple of luxury couches in the seating area where suited businesspeople tapped away on laptops and swilled coffee.

"Thank you," said Roxy. Nat was already walking away. When Roxy sat down, she found herself fidgeting. She drummed her fingers against the leather arms of her chair.

"I don't know where I'm going to go either," Roxy said quietly. "My boyfriend left me. I have no job to go back to."

Nat looked out over the room to avoid making eye contact with her. "Hmph. You can go stay with your family."

"I don't have any family," Roxy said. "I don't know my dad. And . . . well, my mom and I don't get on."

Nat looked at her then, surprised, as if she were considering Roxy from a whole new perspective. "Oh . . . I thought . . . well, I don't know. You just seem like the kind of person who'd have a wonderful family who loves you, who you could go home to on the holidays, eat massive amounts of food, and have a laugh with."

Roxy chuckled. "I wish!"

Nat frowned and pursed her lips. "Are you sure? You look so . . . normal."

"I do my best," Roxy admitted. "Looks like I'm doing a better job than I thought."

"My parents would love to have a daughter like you," Nat said ruefully. "Unfortunately, they can't stand the sight of me. I'd hate to go back to England with my tail between my legs, deported."

"I know what you mean," Roxy said, feeling a rush of recognition. "Every time something goes wrong, my mom loves to tell me how bad I am at being a grown-up. I haven't told her anything about my job or my boyfriend—*ex*-boyfriend. It would give her too much ammunition. I find it better to say nothing."

"Sounds just like my dad." Nat sighed. "Perhaps we're not quite as different as we look."

"Maybe not," Roxy said. Nat gave her a little smile and leaned over. She held out her fist. Roxy met it with her own—a fist bump! She didn't think she'd ever done one before. It wasn't conventional, but it worked. Their shared experience bonded them together.

Shortly afterward, the receptionist came out of the shining silver elevator in the hotel lobby. "There's no answer from his room," he told Nat. "I'm afraid you'll have to try again later."

At that moment, Nat's phone rung. It was Elijah. Nat put the call on speakerphone. Roxy could hear a voice, it sounded like Louise's, wailing and sobbing in the background.

"This was supposed to be . . . the beginning . . . of my new . . . life!" She sounded hysterical. And no wonder.

For it was Louise, it turned out, who had found the missing property developer. He was in the cemetery at the end of the alleyway, behind one of the graves. He was dead, a bullet through his chest.

Louise had come across Richard Lomas' body on her morning jog. At first, she thought he was passed out drunk and shook him, but . . . "Deathly cold!" she'd reported through sobs. "Deathly cold! And with a gunshot wound!"

Now, Roxy sat in the corner of the dining room at Evangeline's, feeling numb as the drama played out before her. They had raced back to the guest-house from the hotel, and Nat had gone straight into panic mode. She couldn't stop making tea and coffee and plying everyone with beignets. "A cup of tea will make everything better," she kept saying.

"It's her crazy English way," Evangeline explained. She sat slumped in a chair, periodically shaking her head, biting her lip, and wringing her hands. Elijah had rushed over when he heard Louise's screams, and his complexion was now a shade of green that matched his shirt. He hovered in the doorway, looking unsure of himself. In the corner, Sage took Louise in her arms and rocked her gently, stroking her hair to calm her. Slowly,

Louise's wails subsided to sobs, then to a whimper as the shock of her discovery abated.

9-1-1 had been called, and as the small group waited for the police, the friends sat mostly in silence, all quietly contemplating Louise's discovery, what it could mean, and wondering what on earth would happen next.

CHAPTER FOURTEEN

DETECTIVE WILLIAM JOHNSON was a robust man in his early sixties with thick glasses and a bald head. He wasn't particularly tall or large, but he was sturdy and sure on his feet. He somehow dwarfed the dining room. He wore a sharp black suit and had the look of a bull that was about to charge.

As soon as he stepped into the room, Sage shivered. "Bad vibes," Roxy heard her whisper. "Very bad vibes."

Roxy couldn't have agreed more. Johnson seemed to make the very air turn cold and hostile. He was deeply unsettling, and the cruel glimmer in his eyes made Roxy feel like running upstairs and pulling the comforter over her head. As he looked over at Evangeline, Roxy could have sworn she heard him growl.

"Right, listen up! It seems that this was the last place the victim was seen alive." His eyes swiveled to Evangeline. They were beady, threatening. "He was talking to you." Johnson looked back at the others and said, "So you'll all stay here until you've spoken with me one by one."

Sam came running into the dining room, his eyes wild with anxiety. "Elijah called me. Is everyone okay?"

Detective Johnson sneered. "We're all fine, thank you, Superman. But now that you're here, you can sit yourself down, too."

"Right," Sam said, a little defensively. Roxy couldn't help but notice he looked pretty nervous, just as Nat did. Did he have something to hide, too? He avoided Johnson's eyes and rounded his broad shoulders like he was trying to make himself smaller, inconspicuous. "Well, I'm glad everything's being taken care of." Sam sat down on a chair by the door.

"Shall I fix everyone some coffee?" Nat said. When she got no response, "Maybe tea would be better?" She bit her lip and rushed into the kitchen.

"You first," Johnson said, pointing at Roxy.

"M . . . me?" said Roxy.

The detective sneered again. "Yes. You."

"Oh, but I wasn't even here when the body was found. I just came back."

Johnson stared at her. "Roxy Reinhardt, right? I've heard that you were at the victim's *hotel* when the body was found! I want to know why."

He took her to a side room off the lobby, which Evangeline and Nat used as a place to dump stuff in order to keep everywhere else clean. There was a mess of files, some with papers poking out as they tried to make their escape onto the floor. An old washing machine stood in the corner, and an assortment of random items, including napkins, plates, bed linen, and bizarrely, a bicycle wheel, were crammed into the rest of the space.

There was just about enough room for two chairs. Johnson set his recording device on top of a stack of files and sniffed. "Well, this will have to do." He then stated the date and time for the benefit of the recording. "Now please give me your full name."

"Roxanne Melissa Reinhardt," Roxy said.

"Date of birth?"

"2, 27, 1995."

"Address?"

"Well . . . I'm kind of *between* addresses," she said. She really didn't want to elaborate about her breakup to this stern-faced, hard-hearted detective, but he looked at her with one eyebrow cocked. It clearly meant, "explain." She tried to put a positive spin on things. "I'm starting a new life," she said, holding her head high. "I wanted a change of scenery."

"Tell me about what you were doing before and where," Johnson said flatly. She had to go into detail, it seemed. "And how did you end up in New Orleans?" he said when she had finished.

"By bus," she said.

He sighed, exasperated. "No, *why* New Orleans in particular?"

Roxy gulped. What could she say? Because her *cat* had alerted her to a commercial, which had stirred a feeling deep inside her that she didn't understand? And she'd simply abandoned her former life and left? How ridiculous did *that* sound? In fact, it *was* ridiculous. What on earth was she doing with her life?

"Ms. Reinhardt?" Johnson said. He was watching her suspiciously.

She realized she had better come up with an answer fast. "Well, what with my ex-boyfriend leaving and me having a stressful time at work, I was attracted here by the, um, cuisine. It intrigued me. I thought it would be good to go somewhere . . . interesting." Roxy's palms were sweating, but she didn't want to wipe them against her jeans in case it made her look guilty.

"So, you left your job and your home town indefinitely because of . . . Creole and Cajun *food*?" Detective Johnson did not sound impressed. Roxy didn't know if that was because he suspected her of lying, or that he considered her life choices to be ludicrous.

"Something like that, sir."

"Ooookay, then," Johnson said. He continued on. "Richard Lomas died from a gunshot wound in the early hours of this morning. Also this morning, you accompanied . . . someone . . . to the Fontainebleau Hotel where he was staying, in order to track him down. Why was that?"

Roxy could feel her hands trembling. Authority figures always made her feel afraid. "Well . . . " she began, and her voice wobbled. "Evangeline had decided she was going to sell the guesthouse to Mr. Lomas and had arranged for him to come over and sign the papers. He didn't turn up. The atmosphere here was tense, and I decided a walk would do me good. So when Nat said she was going to find him, Mr. Lomas, that is, I decided on the spur of the moment to go with her. Evangeline was angry that he hadn't shown up."

"Right," the detective said. "Evangeline is a well-known figure in these parts. She's been part of the establishment for decades. What is not clear is why she would decide to sell to this developer. She's well-known in town as a conservationist, wanting to keep old buildings alive. She's also known as someone who never gives up, even in the face of a sensible, logical proposition." The veins in Johnson's temples stood out, and his jaw muscle twitched as a dark cloud of annoyance swept over his face as he spoke. Roxy got the feeling there was some history between the two that she didn't know about. His animosity seemed extreme and out of place for so early in an investigation. "I find it hard to believe she would sell her property knowing that he would tear it down and develop the area beyond all recognition."

"I think she's at the end of her rope," Roxy said. "Exhausted by the responsibility and drudgery of running such a place. I'm sure she didn't do it if that's what you mean. Kill Mr. Lomas," Roxy blurted out. "I mean, why would she? She wanted to sell her property to him."

Johnson smirked. "Is that so? Well, thank you for that important insight. Tell me again, which police department did you transfer from to come here?"

CHAPTER FIFTEEN

"I . . . UH . . ." ROXY stumbled.

"So who do *you* think did it?" Johnson said, leaning forward, his eyes bright, his voice full of fake enthusiasm. He was mocking her.

Roxy felt heat flush her cheeks. A sense of shame burned in her chest, but since she'd been asked the question, she decided to answer it. "Probably Mara Lomas. That's his wife. She came over yesterday, telling us to inform her husband that she knew what he was doing. Something about an affair."

"Right," Johnson said, raising his eyebrows and looking a little more interested in what she had to say. "She came over here?"

"Yes, she was in the street outside."

"That's mighty convenient for Evangeline," he muttered under his breath. He coughed and looked down at his notebook. When he looked back up at Roxy, his eyes were shining.

His expression sent a shiver through Roxy. What *was* his beef with Evangeline? Did he hold a grudge against her? He wasn't being logical, that was for sure. Or without bias, it would seem.

"Not convenient at all," Roxy said firmly. "How would killing Lomas help her? His wife has a far stronger motive." Roxy wasn't quite sure where she was finding the courage to speak out like this, but her sense of fair play was acute. And justice wasn't being done here.

"I'm not interested in your speculation," Johnson snapped, despite the fact he had been asking for just that a minute or so ago.

A silence stretched out between them. Roxy played with her fingers in her lap while Johnson sat back and let out a sigh. Roxy doubted he ever felt uncomfortable. He had far too much confidence and self-assurance. It was very off-putting.

"Is this place going to be shut down?" she asked.

"Not yet," Johnson said with a snort. "There's no reason for it. However, if a certain someone happens to be guilty and is carted off to jail, it won't be able to continue. It will have to be sold, probably to another developer who will tear it down. No one will buy it and retain it in its current state." He looked around with disgust as if he had found himself in a stinking pigpen.

"Actually, two people said they would buy it, aside from the developer."

"And you tell me that *now?*" Detective Johnson said, leaning forward. "Who? We may have to protect them from . . ." Roxy knew he *desperately* wanted to say Evangeline, but he couldn't, because the tape was running. "Harm," he said eventually. "Give me their names."

"Louise, the other guest," Roxy said. "The one who found the body. She's an interior designer. And Sam, the handyman and laundryman. He plays the saxophone," she added and regretted it immediately. The instrument Sam played was completely irrelevant to the inquiry.

"Okay," Johnson said. "We need to make sure they stay safe. They might be in danger. Are either of them putting pressure on Evangeline to sell?"

"I don't think so," Roxy said. "They seemed to be offering a way to preserve the building and for Evangeline to stay on in some capacity. They didn't want to tear it down. They wanted to keep the guesthouse as is, improve it, update it. Their offers seemed to be acts of genuine kindness."

Detective Johnson opened his eyes wide and shook his head slowly. Roxy stopped herself from speaking. He was still being illogical. There was no sane reason to suspect Evangeline. "Right," he said. "So you would say they're on Evangeline's side?"

Roxy was getting a little sick of his line of questioning. He seemed so closed-minded, so dogged in his dislike of Evangeline. Every time he said her name his lip literally curled. "I don't know," she said, a little more sharply than she'd usually have managed toward an authority figure. "I'm new around here. I don't know anything about sides."

"Whatever," he said. His voice thickened into a monotonous drawl and his eyes glazed over as he said, "Can you account for your whereabouts last night?"

Roxy explained about the parade, then the meal, and the boat ride. She told him of her near mugging, and how afraid she had been, and how Sam had come to her rescue.

"Why are you going red?" Detective Johnson said.

That only made her blush deeper, and stammer for the right words to say. "It's . . . it's hot in here."

Johnson rolled his eyes. "Can you tell me what Evangeline was doing last night? Was she with you at the parade? At the meal? On the boat ride?"

"No," Roxy said. "She stayed here. She said she'd been to enough carnival parades to last a lifetime, and she didn't feel like it. I think she was very sad. She seemed to have resigned herself to selling this guesthouse, but she doesn't really want to."

"Conjecture," Detective Johnson snapped. "You have no idea what she was thinking. And she was here, alone, not far from where the victim was found. Very suspicious."

"Well, I do know that she was holding Nefertiti when we left. Nefertiti's a very good companion when you're not feeling your best. And she's a very good judge of character."

"Who on earth is Nefertiti?" Johnson said irritably.

"My cat."

Johnson smirked. "And we can trust your cat to be a reliable character witness, can we?" He rolled his eyes again. "Anything more to say?"

"I don't think so," Roxy said. She couldn't stand being around this guy. She wanted to get away from him as quickly as possible. Roxy burned to say something to him about how he was assuming all kinds of bad things about Evangeline, but a shadowy fear swirled within her and sucked her voice down her throat. She lost her nerve. She wasn't brave or bold enough.

"No," Roxy said eventually, more firmly this time.

"Right. Interview over." Johnson snapped off the machine. "Now, I want to see the girl you went to the hotel with, whatever her name is; the strange looking one who works here, the one with all the tattoos, wears only black."

"That's Nat." Roxy felt for Nat. She was going to sweat. Roxy hoped Nat was a good actress because before she had even blinked, Johnson would have decided that her close relationship with Evangeline meant Nat was probably an accomplice to some crime that existed only in his mind. And that was before he knew of her illegal status.

"Nat," Johnson said disapprovingly. "Go and get her. And tell her to bring me some coffee and beignets. And don't scrimp on the beignets, you hear?"

CHAPTER SIXTEEN

"THAT GUY," NAT said furiously. "Who the heck does he think he is?"

"Right?" Roxy agreed.

"He is deeply entrapped by his ego," Sage said. "His true self is lost somewhere so deep within him that he doesn't know who he is."

"Well, I know exactly *what* he is," said Nat. "A complete and utter . . ."

"He thinks Evangeline's the murderer," Roxy said, cutting Nat off before she said something she might regret. "And seemingly without any evidence."

After Johnson had finished speaking with her, Roxy had watched the others, Nat, Evangeline,

Louise, Elijah, Sage, and briefly, Sam, go into the small junk room one by one. They had all traipsed out again a while later, their faces blank. Judging by the look on the detective's face when he finally emerged, no one, it seemed, had had any information that was remotely useful.

In need of a break, Roxy, Sage, and Nat had decided to take a walk down by the Mississippi River. Sage had said she was feeling "energetically tied up" and Roxy knew exactly what she meant. The African-American woman looked particularly serene that morning, in long, flowing robes the color of golden sunlight. She had pulled back her now-braided mermaid hair into a topknot and adorned it with yellow-gold flowers. They were real, Roxy could tell, the petals had begun to droop a little.

"Of course it wasn't Evangeline," Nat snapped. "It's *got* to be the developer's wife."

"That's what I told him as well," said Roxy. "She's got to be the main suspect, surely?" Then an idea struck her. "Sage?" she said, then paused because she realized the idea sounded silly.

Sage looked at her. "What is it, good soul?"

"I don't know . . . this sounds kind of dumb." Roxy wasn't afraid to say it in front of Sage, but she *was* scared of Nat's reaction. Sniggering was the most likely one.

"Go ahead," Sage said smoothly. She gave Nat a warning look. Roxy wondered if Sage's skills included mind reading.

She blew out a little breath and looked over the river. She tried to find a way to phrase what she was about to say so that it didn't sound preposterous. "You know that you know magic and everything . . . ?"

"Yes," Sage said, her face lighting up.

"Like the cards and stuff. I was wondering if there was any way to . . . well, to find out who did it. Using magic."

"Oh, come on, Rox," said Nat. Sage shot her another look, but it didn't stop her. "If that were the case, we wouldn't need detectives or police or anything. Sage isn't Harry Potter, you know, and this is New Orleans, not Hogwarts."

"I know, but . . ." Roxy struggled to reply. She knew it was a crazy idea.

"Well, good friends, there *are* ways to do so," said Sage, mellow despite Nat's derision. "But it requires very advanced magic. I have been practicing for thirty-three years, and even I wouldn't trust my own ability at that level. Magic of that form is . . . complex."

"Then who would be able to do it?" Roxy asked. "Can we find someone like that?"

"It would need to be one who has trained with a long line of indigenous priests, perhaps an advanced magician from Haiti or the Congo, or somewhere deep in the heart of South America. Certainly not me, unfortunately."

"Oh, what rubbish!" Nat said. "You don't really *believe* in all this magic stuff, do you, Sage? Sure, you mess around with the cards and buy your lotions and potions and incense. But it doesn't really *mean* anything, does it? It's just a source of comfort, a hobby. It's not *real*."

"That is grossly disrespectful, Nat," Sage said calmly.

"Yeah, but, come on! Magic? Even little kids grow out of that by the time they're 7 or 8. Yet here you are, a grown person, actually professing to believe in this stuff?"

"Everyone believes in different things," Roxy said, trying to smooth the atmosphere over.

"People around the world have used magic for thousands and thousands of years," Sage said. "Since the beginning of time. Whole societies have depended upon it. Look at the Ancient Egyptians, for example."

"Why would I do that?" Nat said dismissively.

Roxy looked up to the sky.

To her surprise, Sage actually laughed gently.

"You haven't done any in-depth research into magic throughout the ages, have you?" she asked Nat.

"No, I have not," Nat retorted.

"Have you read a single book on magic?"

"Well, no, but . . ."

"Exactly," Sage said smoothly. "You're simply projecting your uneducated prejudice onto me, without even knowing what you're talking about. And we are supposed to be friends, Nat. You're devaluing the foundation of my entire existence. That is *not* what friends do."

Roxy found her heart beating faster. "I don't think she meant to . . ."

"Nat knows exactly what she's doing," said Sage, her voice getting harder. The light caught her eyes and Roxy could see tears reflected in them. "Magic is my life. Magic saved me from . . . well, let's say I haven't had the easiest life. Magic is why I'm here today." Nat dropped her head and stared at her combat boots.

"And because Nat is stressed about this situation and her own *precarious* status, she starts picking a fight with me to let off some steam." Sage drew herself up to her full height. She was nearly six-feet tall. "Hear this, Nat. You need to be more aware of your feelings and be honest about them. The more you hide and suppress them, the more they come out in toxic leaks like this. You have hurt me with your words, very deeply. But I will choose the higher road." Her voice wobbled. "I'll see you all later." Sage glided away, her golden robes swishing.

CHAPTER SEVENTEEN

ROXY COULD HEAR her heart beating against her chest. She and Nat walked on in silence, neither of them wanting to talk about what had just happened. Soon they found a bench, and Nat flopped down on it. Roxy joined her. They both stared across the rippling river for a while.

"She's right, you know," Nat said eventually. "I am worried about being found out and deported *and* this whole murder thing. I knew what I was saying was hurtful, but there was something in me that just kept pushing on and on, wanting to keep going until she got mad at me. But Sage never gets mad. Not really."

Roxy couldn't understand what Nat was talking

about. The idea of riling someone up until they got upset seemed both pointless and abhorrent to her.

"Now she's gone off, I feel kind of relieved," Nat said. "But also horrible. Because she's really upset now."

"Maybe you could go after her and apologize?" Roxy suggested. "She's probably at the magic store."

"How ironic," Nat said, shaking her head.

Roxy watched a cloud being carried by the wind through the cold, blue sky. "Do you really believe what you said about magic?"

Nat sighed. "I don't know. Like Sage said, I don't know anything about it, really. I guess I'm a skeptic, but I haven't looked into it. Not properly. It just seems so, oh I don't know, pie in the sky, airy-fairy."

"I've never really come across it before," said Roxy. "I don't know if I believe in it, but it is interesting. Since I've been here, I realize there are a *lot* of things I don't know about. My life has been . . . sheltered."

Nat laughed, but not unkindly. "That's why I left England. I was born in London's East End and my parents have worked hard all their lives. They wanted the best for me but our ideas of what that looked like were different. I was expected to go to university, get a clean, respectable office job, get married, have 2.3 kids or whatever, and a mortgage, preferably on a house in the suburbs. To them that was success, but just saying that bores me, let alone *doing* it for the rest of my life."

It sounded lovely to Roxy, but she could appreciate it wasn't for everyone. "You wanted more adventure."

"Yep," said Nat. "I got a nanny job here. My plan was to travel afterward. Go to India. Australia. Thailand." She laughed again, but it was hollow.

"You could still, couldn't you?"

"Yeah, I think so. But since I've overstayed my visa, I'm guessing they'll never let me back into the US once I leave."

"Oh."

"When I do leave or get deported, I'm going to be leaving for good. So, as much as I want to explore the world, I'm not sure I can bring myself . . ." Nat looked around. "New Orleans has become like home to me now. And Evangeline's like . . . not my mum exactly, but oh, I don't know, my crazy great aunt, or something. I don't want Evangeline's to get shut down."

"Me, neither," said Roxy. "I'm already feeling attached to the place, and I've only been here a couple of days."

Nat gave a smile tinged with a little sadness. "Sage is very wise," Nat said. "The magic stuff aside, she just *is* magic. She knows a lot of stuff. Before I met her, I'd *never* be here talking to you about emotions and stuff. I'd be somewhere down there . . ." She pointed to a bridge. "Probably *under* there, drinking away my sorrows, sure that no one would understand, and that I was the only person in the world with problems." She laughed at herself. "Sage is very wise," she repeated.

Roxy smiled. "She does seem like a very special person."

"Yep," Nat said. She got up from the bench. "Let's go find her, and I can tell her what a total idiot I am."

Roxy stood and gave Nat a side hug. "You're not a total idiot."

"Oh, really I am," Nat said raising her eyebrows.

"We need to make a plan," Roxy said firmly. "A plan of how we're going to find out who *really* killed that developer. I feel sure Johnson will try to pin the murder on Evangeline, and that'll ruin everything as well as be a terrible miscarriage of justice." Roxy felt a great sense of loyalty toward these people already. "If he isn't going to investigate fairly, then *we* will."

Nat looked at Roxy in surprise. "You're feistier than I thought," she said.

Roxy smiled back, remembering something her old English teacher had said. He'd been the only teacher who hadn't treated her as if she were invisible. *Roxy, you're soft on the outside, but steely underneath, where it counts.* Roxy had never believed him but now, she felt it. It was a rush. "Thanks," she said to Nat.

CHAPTER EIGHTEEN

SAGE TOOK NAT'S bumbling apology outside the magic supplies store very graciously. In fact, she threw her arms around Nat's shoulders and squeezed her tight. "You know I love you, don't you, honey?"

Nat sniffed and swallowed hard. She bent her head into Sage's robed shoulder. She was the type to hold back tears at all costs, stiff upper lip and all that. "Yep," was all she could manage.

As they walked their way back to Evangeline's, the silence between them was companionable and restful after the emotional drama of earlier. The air was cold, but Roxy found it exhilarating. It chilled her cheeks as clouds cast a dark canopy over them, threatening rain. Sage had bought some strongly fragranced incense and even unlit, its mysterious musky smell wafted up from the paper bag she held and made the air around them sweet and unusual.

As they walked through the streets of the city, past a mixture of old, traditional buildings and flashing neon signs, Roxy felt something that she never had before. A sense of purpose, perhaps? *A mission*? A quest? But not only that . . . she felt a kinship. A *shared* goal. It struck her as she fell into step beside Nat and Sage.

For the first time, Roxy felt like she belonged. She felt like she mattered, that she was part of something bigger than herself. She stopped thinking in any sort of longing, tugging way about her ex-boyfriend. Instead, she wondered, "What on *earth* was I thinking?" And, quite miraculously, she stopped worrying and desperately craving security and stability. It was ironic that here, in a city she didn't know, with people she had just met, in an accommodation that could fall through at any moment, with the most uncertain future she had ever faced, she felt the safest she ever had.

Finally, Nat spoke up as they walked past a diner, and the air around them became thick and warm with the forceful smell of burgers and fries. It was so strong; it even drove away the scent of the incense that permanently swirled around Sage. "Oh heck, I'm starving," Nat said. "Let's grab some lunch here." She slipped her phone out of her pants pocket. "It's two o'clock already. I doubt Evangeline will be up to cooking today. I'm certainly not."

Sage, a vegetarian, ordered herself a portion of fries. Nat got a cheeseburger, fries and a milkshake. Roxy, meanwhile, realized that she'd barely nibbled at her beignets that morning, and there was a dull ache in her stomach. The events of the day had distracted her, but as whiffs of fast food assailed her, her hunger made itself known, and she felt slightly nauseous. She ordered a chicken burger and fries combo that came with a soda. The food arrived in minutes, and they carried their trays to one of the laminated tables. It was safe to say this was not one of New Orleans' finest eating establishments, but Roxy didn't care. Right then, something cheap, familiar, and fattening seemed the best option.

None of them said much until their food was mostly eaten. Roxy's mind wandered back to the case. "How are we going to prove to Johnson that the murderer is not Evangeline? I'm *sure* it's Mara Lomas. I mean, come on, she thought her husband was having an affair, and she *threatened* him—out loud and in public. She said he needed all the protection he could get. How on earth can Johnson think it was Evangeline with that evidence in front of him? It's a total open and shut case."

"One would think so," Sage said with a grimace.

"But knowing the story between that man and Evangeline, I wouldn't be so sure."

"Aha! I *knew* there had to be a history between them!" Roxy exclaimed. "When he questioned me, he was acting like he loathed her. Why is that?"

Sage blew a stream of air out of her mouth and adjusted her golden robes. "Evangeline's always been quite an activist. That lady is *tough*, I tell you. When she believes in something and knows she's right, she'll hang on to the very end. It's actually most unlike her to have given in to this developer. It's sad, really. I think it's because her eyesight is deteriorating, but anyway, she's been a thorn in Johnson's side for years."

"In what sense?" Roxy asked.

"Hey!" Nat interrupted. "Look!"

Roxy turned to see Nat pointing at the TV on the wall. It was showing local news. *MURDER*, it read at the bottom of the screen. There was a female reporter standing in front of the cordoned-off cemetery. Blue lights flashed. Police swarmed everywhere behind her.

"Hey, would you turn it up, please?" Nat said to the young woman behind the counter.

The woman pressed her lips together and flicked her mousey brown ponytail with annoyance, but she complied with Nat's request. It was an old-fashioned boxy television, and the woman, who was quite short, had to reach up on tiptoes to press the volume button.

"The wife of the deceased is currently assisting police with their investigations," the reporter said, her hair blowing about her in the breeze.

"Aha!" Nat took a delighted sip on her milk-shake, her eyes lighting up. "Well, there we go. Johnson has seen sense after all. 'Assisting with investigations' *always* means guilty as heck. It's just that they're not quite ready to charge her."

Roxy had been imagining Evangeline rattling around in jail, the other prisoners taking advantage of her as her eyesight got worse. She frowned as she sipped on her straw, even though her soda was long drained. "I certainly hope you're right," she said.

CHAPTER NINETEEN

THEY CONTINUED TO stare at the TV even though the news report had moved on to more upbeat topics. The channel was now showing footage of the carnival celebrations.

"You know, I don't think Mara did it," Sage said.

"Of course she did," Nat scoffed.

But Roxy wasn't so quick to dismiss Sage. "What makes you say that?"

Sage looked straight at Roxy, her dark eyes flashing. "My intuition."

"Oh, for goodness . . ." Nat began, then seemed to remember their earlier argument and rushed to say, "Well, I mean, well, you know, I . . ." She couldn't find anything with which to elegantly finish off her sentence so she sighed and her shoulders slumped. "Sorry."

"Not to worry, sugar," Sage said. She threw Nat a wink and patted her hand.

Roxy's mind began to whir again. She had never *ever* trusted her intuition. In the past, she'd always felt too anxious to *have* any. Her decision to come to New Orleans had been unique in that respect. Until that point, when faced with choices, Roxy had always gone for the safest option, the one with the least potential to go wrong. Now, however, feeling much more relaxed in New Orleans among her new friends, the strange gut feeling she had, the fluttering that told her, *No, something isn't quite right here,* stood out. She wondered what it could mean. If Mara hadn't killed the developer, then who had?

"Let's go," Nat said. "Now that they've caught that dead man's crazy wife, maybe Evangeline will think about keeping the guesthouse open. I want to persuade her."

"You know she can't afford to keep it going," said Sage, as they tipped their tray contents into the trash. "It's been running at a loss for ages."

"Yeah, but Sam said he'd buy it off her," Nat said breezily as if the deal had already been sealed. "And Louise is our backup. As annoying as she is, if she keeps the guesthouse open, I'll be her best friend for life."

Roxy laughed. "And maybe there'll finally be a steamy romance between her and Sam as they run the guesthouse together. It'd be like something out of a book."

Nat snorted. "In her dreams."

"She's alright," Roxy said as they walked back out onto the street.

"No, too old, too cougar," said Nat. "And she keeps totally embarrassing herself."

"She is suffering," Sage said. "I would say both her first and second chakras are severely out of balance."

Nat opened her mouth, then closed it again. She let out a huge happy sigh, swinging her arms as they walked. "Well, looks like that dumb Johnson won't be sniffing around for much longer. Let's go home and persuade Evangeline and Sam and Louise or any combination of the above to keep Evangeline's open."

When they got back, they found that Evangeline was not in the mood to be persuaded to do anything, however. They found her sweeping the dining room and humming a furious tune, her lips pursed tightly together. Roxy saw her roughly wipe away a tear from her cheek.

Sam was in the corner bagging up tablecloths for laundering. He gave Nat a cautionary look as they walked in, but Nat ignored him.

"Did you see Mara Lomas has been arrested, Evangeline? We're all off the hook. You can relax. So promise me you're going to keep this place, and I won't get deported."

"She's not been arrested, just taken in for questionin'," Evangeline said, not looking up from her sweeping. "And your immigration status has nothin' to do with me. I helped you out when I didn't have to, so I don't appreciate you tryin' to put a guilt trip on me, Miss Natalie."

"*Don't* call me that," said Nat. All the confidence had seeped out of her voice.

"Now, there's things to do," said Evangeline, "and you've been out for far too long. You can begin by tacklin' that stack of teacups in the kitch'n."

Nat pressed her lips together and walked away to make a start on the cups, accompanied by a lot of banging and slamming.

Evangeline sighed. "I'm being horrible, aren't I?" she said to Sage.

Sage placed a hand on her arm and said in a quiet, kind voice. "Perhaps you're not quite embodying your best self."

Evangeline burst into tears. "I'm sorry, Nat, cher," she said, going to the kitchen door and speaking through it. "I'm just so very upset about the guesthouse and if everythin's goin' to work out. Don't take old Evangeline so seriously. Don't take my words to heart, cher."

Evangeline pushed the door open and went into the kitchen, wrapping a surprised Nat up in a big, warmly reciprocated hug. Roxy and Sage exchanged glances. Despite their bickering back and forth, Nat and Evangeline were clearly quite fond of one another. But, oh the tension. Roxy was fit to wilt.

CHAPTER TWENTY

AFTER THE SECOND emotional reconciliation in as many hours, Roxy needed a break. She headed to her room. Nefertiti was on the stairs, attending to her complex self-grooming regimen. As soon as she saw Roxy, she sprang to her feet and wound her fuzzy, fluffy self round and round Roxy's ankles.

"Hello, beautiful girl," Roxy said, leaning down to tickle her under the chin.

Nefertiti purred loudly, then padded up the stairs alongside her owner.

"You like it here, don't you?" said Roxy before sighing emphatically. "Me too. I'm going to find a way to get us to stay here, Nef." She turned to look at Nefertiti's cute squashed up face. "We might have to do a little investigating, though. Oh, oh!" Roxy suddenly found herself knocked off her feet as she turned the corner of the stairs and fell sprawling across the staircase.

"Oh no!" Louise said. "Sorry!" Her voice was thick as if she had been crying. She was sitting on the stairs looking out of one of the old stained glass windows, her knees pulled up under her chin.

"It's okay," Roxy said, grabbing onto the stair rail to pull herself up. "I wasn't looking where I was going."

Louise wiped mascara from under her eyes, where it had begun to run in black streaks carried by her tears. "Are you hurt?"

"No," Roxy said, although her elbow ached a little where she'd banged it against a step. "Are you?"

"I'm fine," said Louise. She even tried a smile, but it looked so strained, hiding so much pain, that it tugged at Roxy's heart.

Roxy felt a little nervous at what she was about to do and tapped one hand into the palm of the other. In the past, she had always diverted herself from any drama or problem or worry as soon as she could. Anything that wasn't completely smooth sailing made her bite her lip and her pulse race. But this time, things felt different. She needed to do something.

Roxy sat down next to Louise and put an arm around her. "Something's up. What's wrong?"

Nefertiti clearly thought Louise had a lot of wrong going on, because she curled up at the feet of the two women and tucked her head under her paw, falling quickly into a snooze.

Louise looked down at the cat and gave a sad little smile. "She looks so cozy and happy and safe."

Roxy smiled. "She sure does."

Louise let out a long, sad sigh. "I wish I felt like that."

"It would be awesome to be a cat, wouldn't it?" Roxy agreed.

That made Louise laugh a little, her voice still tinged with sadness. "Life would be a whole lot less complicated, that's for sure."

They sank into silence. Roxy looked at Louise out of the corner of her eye, trying to read her expression. "Is it . . . just that . . . well, you've been through so much already, what with your husband having an affair, you feeling like you had a new life ahead, and then this awful . . ." She couldn't bring herself to say the word. "This awful *thing* happened. You must be feeling like you don't know what to do and that things are hopeless anyway."

Louise widened her eyes. "Are you psychic? You read me like a book, Roxy. That's incredible."

"Oh, gosh," Roxy said quickly, flushing with

embarrassment at the compliment. "No special skills here at all. I . . . I think it's quite easy to see."

Louise burst into tears. "So it's obvious to everyone that I'm a total mess?" she said thickly.

"Oh, no, no!" said Roxy. "That isn't what I meant at all!"

Louise gulped down tears, her face flushing. "Sorry, I apologize," she said. "I really do. A fully grown woman blubbing all over the place like this, it isn't dignified." She pulled herself up straight and attempted to regain her composure, but her face crumpled. "But you're right, it's just like you said. I had thought that this was to be my new start. But . . ."

"Didn't you say you wanted to buy the guest-house?" Roxy said. "You still could. It would be a new start. A new life."

"I'm not sure I want to anymore. I can't . . ." Louise's eyes took on a glazed-over, faraway look as she trailed off.

"You can't what?"

"I can't stop . . . thinking about it. That moment."

Roxy paused for a second to fathom what Louise was talking about. From the traumatized look on her face, she gathered she must have meant the moment she stumbled across Richard Lomas' body.

"It's going to haunt me forever," Louise said. "His eyes . . . his eyes . . . they were open." Roxy shuddered involuntarily. "I want to get away," said Louise, firmly.

"You can do that," Roxy said. "You came here out of nowhere, didn't you say? Just like me. So you could go somewhere else. Anywhere."

Louise shook her head. "It's not the same anymore." Roxy could see she'd lost her confidence, her sense of adventure, her *joie de vivre*. "But I don't want to stay here, either," Louise added. "Anyway, I can't get away from myself, can I? I can't get away from what's in my own mind."

Roxy sighed. There was no answer to that. "I guess not." She was starting to feel a little depressed herself. She tried to come up with a positive thought. "Still, at least they've taken Mara Lomas, the developer's wife, in for questioning. That's progress, isn't it?"

"I guess," Louise said, looking unsure. "If she really is the killer. But it could have been . . ." She opened her mouth, and then closed it suddenly again. "Well, it could have been anyone."

Roxy's heart started thumping a little louder than usual. She looked at Louise. "Do you have an idea who the murderer might be?"

CHAPTER TWENTY-ONE

LOUISE PAUSED. HER eyes flickered. She was weighing something up in her mind. Eventually, she said, "No. We can all make our guesses, I'm sure. But I'd prefer the police find out who did it from the evidence."

"Yes," Roxy agreed. "You're absolutely right."

"But considering Lomas wanted to take over Evangeline's, as well as *other buildings*, and he didn't do business in a very honorable fashion from what I hear, they've probably got a massive suspect pool to work through."

"He wanted to buy up other buildings in the city?"

"Uh-huh," Louise said. "Before you arrived, I found him outside Evangeline's making a phone call. I heard him say something like 'I'm taking a look at two in the French Quarter, then I'll head over to Touro.'"

"Oh," said Roxy. She sat with that information for a moment and let it run through her mind. "Okay." Things seemed to be getting quite a lot more complicated all of a sudden. She slumped back against the stair feeling crushed.

Why on earth had she thought that *she* could find out who the killer was? After all, she was only an ex-call center operator? What did she know about investigations? What did she know about *anything*?

"Well . . ." she said, her mind a blank. "Right."

"Are you going to be staying on here?" Louise asked. "Or do you think you'll move on?"

"I . . . I'm not sure."

"Go out and see the world while you can, would be my advice," said Louise. "Whatever you do, don't settle down with a no-good man and waste half your life, like me." She gave a half-smile. "Hopefully, by the time you're my age, you'll have life a lot more figured out than I do."

Roxy tried to think of a way to respond to her politely, but there wasn't one. She just nodded a little awkwardly instead.

As if sensing the mood, Nefertiti got up and

arched her back in a stretch. She began to pad up the stairs without so much as a backward look.

"It's been such a long day," Roxy said. "I'm going to see if I can nap the rest of the afternoon away."

"That sounds like a good plan," said Louise, offering her another small smile. She remained seated and watched, her eyes soulful and sad, as Roxy stood and followed her cat up the stairs.

Once they entered the loft, Roxy fed Nefertiti a packet of cat food and stood over her as she scarfed it down. When her cat had eaten her fill and raised her head to indicate she was done, Roxy dropped backward onto the bed.

She hadn't realized how tired she was until she sprawled out, her arms and legs spread like a starfish. She looked up at the white ceiling.

The next thing she knew, she awoke with a jerk. It was nighttime—the curtains were drawn, and there was a warm, cozy glow flooding the room. Someone had turned the lamp on. There was the most delicious smell—hearty and spicy and savory and warm.

Against the wall, Roxy saw Evangeline illuminated by the lamp. "Sorry to wake you, cher," she said. "I brought you your dinner. Thought you might like to have it up here. Sage had a tarot reading to do for a client. Nat's gone to listen to her music, and Louise is in her room with a bottle of brandy. So there's no dinner downstairs tonight."

"Sure," Roxy said, feeling quite disoriented as she sat up. "I'd love to have it up here. It smells delicious."

"Awright, cher." Evangeline brought the tray over from the side table and placed it on Roxy's lap. "It's real Creole comfort food. Red beans and rice with sausage and a glass of red wine." Roxy looked down and inhaled its spicy fragrance. "And then some Bananas Foster for dessert. To you, that's bananas browned in a whole heap of butter, sugar, and liquor, and served with vanilla ice cream. My momma used to make that for us as a real treat when I was growin' up. I always like to have it when things aren't so good. Reminds me of her, and how kind she was."

Roxy smiled. "That story will make me enjoy it all the more."

"Well, cher, I'll leave you to your meal. I'll come up later for your tray. Just you leave it outside your door."

Roxy's mind, still dazed from her nap, spun as she tried to formulate a question. "Um, Evangeline?" There was so much to ask. Was she still going to sell the guesthouse? Did Roxy need to find somewhere else to go? Would Nat get deported? Roxy looked up at the ceiling as she deliberated which question to lead with. As she did so, more questions popped into her mind. Why did Johnson dislike Evangeline so much? Why was Richard Lomas looking at other properties? Who did Evangeline believe the murderer to be? Was it her? Roxy's thoughts tied themselves in knots. She didn't really think Evangeline was the killer, but there was a part of her that knew no one could be trusted, not for sure. She had learned that growing up.

Evangeline laughed, as the silence stretched out. "Cat got your tongue?"

"What are you thinking about doing now?" Roxy blurted out.

"I can't say I'm sure yet," Evangeline said. "I *was* set on giving all this up." She cast her eyes around the room. "After all, my eyesight isn't what it used to be, and I don't have the energy I once had. I was all ready to sell to that developer fella, but it would be a real shame to let this place go, especially to have it torn down. Not many appreciate its beauty. She's an old girl, like me, but with a good structure, also like me." Evangeline laughed. "Yet, money is always . . . well, we don't have a money tree out front, do we?"

Roxy said, "I'm not sure Louise is still interested in taking it over, but what about Sam? Maybe he could put some money in the place and help renovate it. Then you would get more customers."

Evangeline's eye's hardened. "Charity, that would be." Her voice had hardened, too. "And Evangeline don't do charity." She bent down and gave Nefertiti a little tickle under her chin. "Ain't she so sweet? Yes, you are, cher! Yes, you are!" she said, cooing now. Roxy couldn't help but smile.

"Goodnight, Roxy. Enjoy your food, cher," the elderly woman said.

"Thanks, Evangeline. For everything."

The guesthouse owner paused by the door and looked back at Roxy with kindness in her eyes. "You're most welcome, cher."

CHAPTER TWENTY-TWO

BREAKFAST THE NEXT morning was another somber affair. Rain pounded at the windows. Outside, the light was a murky gray so dark they had to turn the lamps on. Roxy felt in limbo, and it seemed everyone else felt the same. Nobody spoke, except for Roxy when she gave Nat her order. Nat hadn't even asked her for it. She'd just turned up at the table and raised her eyebrows.

The silence remained unbroken until Elijah burst in with his cases of beignets. "Good morning!" he said jovially, walking across the room at a clip. Then he took in the atmosphere and stopped. "Well, we're a bunch of happy campers today, aren't we?" He laughed. "Don't you know? Today's the Endymion parade!"

He emphasized his words with an excited flourish that was remarkable given how many boxes of pastries he was balancing in one hand. No one replied except Roxy, who felt obliged to say something. She could only come up with a quiet, "Oh, okay."

"The weather's due to clear up by the afternoon. And the place'll be full of kids and laughter and lots of bright colors and fun," he said. "Come on, we all deserve some relaxation time. It will be a distraction."

"There is a time for everything indeed," Sage said. She had popped in for breakfast as she often did, but today she looked run down, in comparison to her usual unruffled self. Her long mermaid hair looked unkempt. Even her robe didn't look right—the linen was all creased, and she'd spilled a drop of orange juice down the front. "Sometimes mourning and solemnity claim time for their own. We cannot always rush to distract ourselves from . . ."

"Oh, come now," Elijah said with a charming smile. "Let's take our minds off all the unpleasantness."

Sage opened her mouth, but quickly closed it and sighed. She resumed munching on her beignet, poring over her laptop.

As he walked past her, Louise shot Elijah a spiteful look. It was so nasty that Roxy was startled by it. After a moment Louise looked down at her oatmeal and stirred her spoon slowly around the bowl. She clearly lacked an appetite. Roxy didn't have one either, but that look perturbed her. Sure, Elijah could be a little insensitive to a mood, a little over the top, but Louise's expression wasn't one of annoyance, it was of pure hatred.

"What d'ya say, Nat? Evangeline?" Elijah said as he went into the kitchen.

Roxy turned back to Louise and scanned her face. The dark cloud had not left her features.

"We're not quite in the right mood for a parade, are we?" Roxy tried.

"Mmmm," Louise said. She was lost in her thoughts.

Roxy pressed on. "And you certainly don't look in the mood for fun."

"Oh, me?" said Louise. "I'm just thinking about liars, and how much I despise them."

They heard Elijah in the kitchen. Louise shot more daggers in his direction.

"Liars?" Roxy said.

"Yes, liars."

Elijah came out of the kitchen and said, "It's settled! We're leaving here at one o'clock after a quick lunch. See you then!"

"Bye," Louise said, in a sickly-sweet voice. She had an equally false smile to match. Her eyes remained cold. As soon as Elijah had turned his back, she grimaced, her face full of disgust. "I hate liars, Roxy."

Roxy leaned in. "What has Elijah lied about?" she asked quietly.

"Oh, not him in particular," Louise said. She leaned back in her chair and her voice lost its intensity, but she couldn't quite meet Roxy's eyes. Roxy would have put money on the fact that Louise was lying. "Just men in general."

"Is Elijah a cheat?" Roxy asked. "Does he even have a partner?"

"What does it matter?" Louise said. "Men are all cheaters and liars as far as I can tell. My husband, your boyfriend, Richard Lomas . . . and all the rest of them."

"I really don't think that's true," said Roxy. "Not all men."

Louise gave her a patronizing smile. "You're still a baby. You probably believe in Prince Charming. That a man will rush in on his charger to rescue you, and you'll both live happily ever after. But don't worry, it'll take a couple more betrayals to knock that belief out of you, but knock it out of you they will."

Roxy felt quite uncomfortable and a little angry

at Louise's condescension. She shifted in her chair and looked at her without flinching. "You were staring at Elijah like you hated him. Why's that?"

Louise raised her eyebrows. "You're imagining things," she said. Her expression softened. "I'm sorry, we're all just tired and cranky and not thinking straight. Let's go to the parade later. I'm going to relax this morning. I suggest you do the same." Without another word, she got up from the table and left.

Roxy sat alone, looking out of the window when, all of a sudden, the lights went out. From the kitchen, the whirring sound of a mixer faded to nothing.

"Oh, for goodness' sake!" Roxy heard Evangeline shout. The old lady came barreling through from the kitchen. "The electricity's gone again," she called over furiously. "The wirin' in this darn place," she said. She shook her head. "No wonder everyone wants to tear it down."

With Evangeline on the warpath, Roxy decided to take Louise's advice. It was a bit early for a nap, but she could escape up to her room for some quiet time. She took a beignet from the table and wrapped it in a napkin, hoping that some of her appetite might return later. Then she headed to the darkened hallway where Evangeline was flicking switches in an electrical box mounted in a closet, still muttering furiously. "Can't even see the darn thing."

"Looks like I arrived at just the right time," a cheery voice called out. They turned to see Sam running into the hallway from the wet cobbled street, ruffling his hair to shake the rain from it. "Hi there, Roxy."

"Hi," said Roxy, a little shyly.

"Electric gone again, Evangeline?"

"No, I just fancied turnin' the lights on and off and rummagin' around in the dark for fun," Evangeline said humorlessly.

"Let me take a look," Sam said with a chuckle.

"I'm goin' back to the kitchen," Evangeline said. She spun on her heel and took off. "Come see me when you've fixed it. I told you this place was falling to pieces."

"Why don't you let me buy . . ."

Evangeline's crotchetiness turned to desperation. She spun around once more to face Roxy and Sam. She looked drained and exhausted. "Please, *stop*," she said. "Please." Then she disappeared into the kitchen.

CHAPTER TWENTY-THREE

SAM GRIMACED BUT moved on quickly. He flashed his phone light on the electrical box, pulled back a panel, and said, "Aha. It's just a couple of wires that need refitting. Evangeline should really do over the whole electrical system, but it's very expensive for a rewire when you have all these period features."

"Ah," Roxy said, wishing she could come out with something insightful, preferably witty. Or at the very least, *interesting*. "I just love the architecture here," was the best she could manage. She hated how simple and uninformed and unsophisticated that sounded. *She* sounded.

"Me too," he said. "Are you busy, Roxy? This is quite a fiddly job. I could pretend I'm some kind of superhero who could do this all by himself, but I just might end up electrocuting myself. Can I ask you to hold a box for me, with my fuses and tools? Then I can easily take what I need without bending down and letting go of a wire? I don't want to start an electrical fire or anything."

"Sure," Roxy said. She noticed that he had blushed a little, plus he was rambling. Perhaps *he* was a little shy, too.

"Thanks," he said. He dashed out into the rain to get tools from his van and quickly returned. "Great. If you could . . . just here would be amazing."

Roxy stood and held her hands out. Sam placed a tray from the inside of his toolbox over her hands and laid various tools and fuses and electrical parts on it like he was performing surgery.

"Right. Perfect," he said. He ducked his head into the electrical box and began to work.

Roxy waited for a moment, before saying, "You've offered to buy this place so many times. Why won't Evangeline take you up on it? Is it really just because she thinks it's charity?"

Sam sighed. "I don't know. I think she thinks I'm, um, humoring her."

"Well, are you?"

"No," he said. Sam looked into her eyes as he leaned over to take a fuse. "I just like things the way they are. Why not keep them the same? I can afford it. And I'd like to help. I've offered to pay for a full rewire in the past. Offered to fix the roof. Take care of the dry rot. But nada. Evangeline won't take any money to keep the place open. She won't take any money to move on. That woman is like a mule. Stubborn as anything. Won't go forward, won't go back." He peered deeply into the fuse box.

"Not to pry, but all these offers you're making sound real expensive. I didn't know the laundry business was quite so lucrative," Roxy said.

Sam's laugh was hollow. "Well, you know . . . life is full of surprises."

Just then, a horrible idea struck Roxy like a lightning bolt. She didn't even know where it came from. It wasn't a result of reasoning or deduction. It was something that flashed through her mind. Was it intuition?

Maybe Sam was getting bankrolled from somewhere. Maybe he used his laundry business as a front to get into all sorts of other "businesses." Perhaps he was a money launderer, buying up failing enterprises to funnel money on from who knows where. Perhaps that's why he was so keen to "help" Evangeline. Maybe *that* was how he got to own a fancy car. Perhaps he'd done this before. Perhaps that's what he'd been hiding all this time!

Roxy didn't know if her imagination was running away with her, or if she was really onto something. But she didn't want the warmth between them to skew her judgment, so she squinted and tried to look at Sam with a cold, objective eye.

He turned to pick another tool from the tray and gave her a lovely smile that drew up one corner of his mouth and showed off a dimple. "That's a real serious face," he said, his eyes dancing with mischief.

Roxy tried to view this, not as charming, but as suspicious and inappropriately irreverent, considering there had just been a murder.

"It appears to me that Detective Johnson will chase Evangeline down as the main suspect," said Roxy. "People say there's a history between them. Do you know what kind of history?"

"Sure, everyone knows," Sam said breezily. "There was a police corruption incident down here about 20 years ago. I was still a little kid back then, but I remember it. It was all over the news. Evangeline organized some major activism around it. You know, sit-ins, protests, that kind of stuff. Johnson was the accused guy's partner. They'd been best friends since childhood. Evangeline's efforts got the guy locked up for a good many years. Well, I should say his crimes are what got him locked up, but he might have gotten away with them if it weren't for her. Johnson has hated her ever since, by all accounts."

"Wow," Roxy said.

"Plus, she's made a lot of fuss over historic buildings getting torn down in the past. She turns up at city hall a lot, speaks at the meetings. She's well-known down there. She makes herself a thorn in certain people's sides, and that doesn't always go down so well. She won't back down and doesn't hesitate to demand what she thinks is right. So Johnson thinks she's somewhere between a menace and a pain in the ass, depending on what mood he's in. They don't see eye to eye at all."

"Do you think he'll try to pin the murder on her?"

Sam paused and looked at her. "I don't know. If he's as corrupt as his former partner, maybe." He laughed. "Though the way Evangeline's going on right now, I wouldn't be so sorry to see the back of her myself."

"Ouch!" Roxy said.

"Bit close to the bone? Yeah, you're probably right, I shouldn't have said it. We all love Evangeline. The place wouldn't be the same without her." Sam fiddled with the electrical box one more time, and the hall lit up.

"Yay!" Roxy said. "Well done."

Sam put on a silly voice and took a bow.

"Thank you. I could not have done it without my assistant, the curious, resourceful, and beautiful Roxanne." He resumed his regular voice. "It is Roxanne, right?"

Roxy wrinkled her nose. "Only to my mom."

"Sorry, Roxy it is then."

They shared a smile.

There was a rustle behind them. Evangeline came rushing in. She squeezed Sam in a hug and kissed him on the cheek. "You're a genius, cher. Don't mind old Evangeline being grouchy. I'm feeling as lost as a polar bear in the Sahara, but that's no excuse. I'm sorry. To you too, Roxy."

"You're not lost," Sam said, smiling at her and squeezing her shoulder. "You're here with us, and you're in exactly the right place."

Roxy watched Sam looking down from his tall height at the diminutive figure of Evangeline and dreaded the idea that he could be faking for his own nefarious reasons. It felt unsettling, viewing someone she liked with suspicion. But years of feeling unsafe had prepared her—she was *well-versed* in not trusting people!

CHAPTER TWENTY-FOUR

IT FELT STRANGE to step out onto the bustling streets that afternoon. People were going about their business as though nothing untoward had happened. Roxy felt she was living in a parallel universe, one that was dark and confusing.

Thankfully, the weather had cleared up. The streets still glistened with the rain of the morning. The sidewalks were covered in watery patches where the blue sky was reflected. But the dark clouds had been chased away by the wind, leaving a cold, clear sky.

In the end, everyone decided to come along to the Endymion parade. Evangeline had taken some persuading; she'd seen a thousand carnivals she said, but Elijah hadn't taken no for an answer. Quite uncharacteristically, she had let herself be swayed. Roxy sidled up to Evangeline as they walked. She was desperate to talk about what Sam had disclosed to her about Evangeline's relationship with Detective Johnson.

"Can I ask you something?" Roxy said, trying to work out how she could phrase it diplomatically.

"Sure."

"Are you worried about Johnson holding a grudge, and trying to pin the murder on you? You know, after what happened." Diplomacy wasn't a skill Roxy possessed it would appear.

But Evangeline wasn't offended. She shook her head. "No. He can try if he likes, the truth will out. I'm innocent, cher. I don't have a motive, and that's that . . . No court would find me guilty." Evangeline peered at her. "How do you know what happened? You're quite the little detective, aren't 'cha?"

"Sam told me," Roxy said. "I think you're brave. I could never do the things he says that you've done."

Evangeline smiled at her. "Of course you could, cher. You may not see it in yourself yet, but there's a whole lot of moxie in there." She tapped the top of Roxy's chest and then laughed. "Moxie Roxy."

Roxy laughed, too.

"He won't try to pin it on me," Evangeline said. "What happened was a long time ago. It's in the past. And Johnson's not corrupt, not like his partner. He might *want* me to be the murderer, but at the end of the day, he's a good cop. We've come to . . . an understandin'. He leaves me alone to run my guesthouse. I leave him alone to do his job. That's all there is to it."

Roxy smiled. "Well, that sounds positive."

"I'm sure it'll be fine, cher. No need to worry yourself about me."

They settled into a comfortable silence.

Slightly ahead of them, Nat clutched a large bottle of iced tea that she swigged from every so often. She looked determined to enjoy herself. Next to her, Sage, in sky-blue robes, sashayed along. Every time a child passed, she gave them a big, kind smile. The children would smile back as they gravitated toward her and away from Louise who was a few steps behind. Louise walked with her head down, her hands thrust into the pockets of her pants, her lips in a flat line. She looked very unhappy. Bringing up the rear, Sam was light on his feet. He listened intently to Elijah. His friend was engrossed in telling a story, jabbing his finger to make his points.

Elijah clutched a huge basket of beignets and had brought another with him that Sam was carrying. "There'll be loads of families out enjoying themselves on St. Charles Avenue," he had explained. "We can sweeten up the occasion!"

Roxy noticed the vibrant shades of purple, green, and gold everywhere—on clothes and flags and decorations and strings of beads hanging around people's necks. One little girl was dressed head to toe in gold. Her dress was gold, her puffy coat was gold, her shoes were gold, her hair bows were gold, and even the beads on her frilly white socks were gold! She wore strings of plastic golden beads around her neck, too. Roxy saw her give Sam a gap-toothed smile as she passed, and he handed her a beignet with a wink.

As they walked along, the dazzling colors of the carnival passing by, Roxy's thoughts took a familiar turn—first they went to her uncertain future, and then they stuck like glue to the unsolved murder. Though she tried to focus on all the fun, sights, and sounds of the carnival, she couldn't help watching each of her party in turn. Were any of them the murderer? And if they were, what might their motivation be?

First, she looked at Evangeline. *Evangeline was desperate for a sale and killed Richard Lomas in a rage over the terms of a deal.* Roxy wondered if it could possibly be true. It probably wasn't, in all likelihood. She couldn't see how Evangeline would benefit from Lomas' death.

They turned onto St. Charles Avenue and into a huge crowd. Kids were raised high, sitting on their fathers' shoulders, waving to people on the parade floats, and squealing with excitement. Music pounded, colors flashed, everyone shouted with excitement. The smells of Creole spices and hot dogs and deep-fried donuts carried on the cold air.

"Woohoo!" Nat said. She took a huge swig from her iced tea bottle.

Nat. *Nat killed Richard Lomas because . . . she knew if Evangeline's closed down, she'd have nowhere to work or live and could be thrown out of the country.* It was a plausible motive. The only thing was that to have killed him, Nat would need to be extremely dark and devious. Roxy hadn't seen any sign of that in her. Hmm. Roxy sure hoped this theory wasn't true, but she knew she had to keep an open mind.

Next, she turned to Louise. Louise was very subdued and serious as she hung back. She was watching the parade without a smile, her expression flat. Roxy could deduce nothing from it.

Louise killed Richard Lomas to . . . Roxy let her imagination click into gear . . . *to get her paws on the guesthouse . . .?* It seemed quite a flimsy reason. Would a middle-aged divorcee have such fire in her belly over a "new life" project that she'd be willing to *murder*? Unlikely, but maybe. People had killed for less.

Roxy looked back at the parade. Folk on the carnival floats were dressed up as all kinds of crazy characters. They tossed sweets and beads and tiny toys into the audience. Little kids scrambled and clutched at them. Many had bags to stuff their trinkets into. One small boy was so adorned with beads that Roxy was surprised he didn't keel over. She watched him as he stuffed his bag full of goodies, grabbing as many as his tiny hands could hold. Older kids hollered, "Throw me something, Mister!" Many adults joined in too, even those as old as Evangeline!

Elijah had given away nearly all his beignets, passing them to any kid nearby who hollered. His grin stretched all over his face. He seemed to be in his element when he was feeding people. Roxy studied him.

Elijah killed Richard Lomas because . . . he wanted to protect his own business? Perhaps . . . perhaps Elijah's bakery wasn't doing so well and it was Evangeline's daily pastry order that was keeping him afloat. If Evangeline's closed down perhaps Elijah's business would, too. By murdering the property developer, Elijah could scupper Evangeline's deal and his bakery business might survive.

Roxy immediately knew this theory was flawed. Elijah made deliveries all over town to various restaurants, hotels, private homes. His business wasn't struggling and in truth, she couldn't see Elijah as a likely suspect. His loud, bright breeziness seemed genuine. But then she thought back to that hateful look Louise had given him earlier. Maybe Louise knew something that Roxy didn't. Her mind began to spin.

"Hey Roxy," Sage said, bobbing up beside her with a grin. "Open your hand."

Roxy put out her palm with a smile, wondering what she was letting herself in for. Sage opened her fist over Roxy's palm, and Roxy looked down to see a pile of glitter in her hand. It was a gorgeous mix of gold and deep purple.

"Fairy dust," Sage explained, opening her eyes wide and looking very serious. "It's collected from special fairy folk in Ireland and contains magical powers."

Roxy looked up into Sage's earnest eyes. "Oh, well, um, thank you."

Sage burst out laughing. "Oh, sugar, I'm having you on! It's just some glittery carnival fun. Though I guess there's no harm in making a wish with it if you want." She winked. "Never any harm in making wishes."

Roxy grinned. "Why not?" Roxy didn't know

what to wish for. She'd never been one for wishing and dreaming. Worrying and procrastinating was more her style. Roxy closed her hand around the glitter and looked at Sage's amused but kind face.

Sage. *Sage killed Richard Lomas because . . .*

CHAPTER TWENTY-FIVE

ROXY TRIED TO work out what Sage would have to lose if Evangeline's was sold off. Not much, it seemed. She did some website work for the elderly guesthouse owner, but that hardly sounded lucrative compared with the corporate clients who were constantly hiring her. In fact, Roxy had a hunch that the work Sage did for the guesthouse was free of charge. Maybe she had another reason, but Roxy doubted it. Besides, Sage was a vegetarian. She didn't even believe in killing *animals*. Roxy was hard-pressed to believe Sage would ever kill a human being. This whole spiritual thing couldn't be an act . . . could it? She looked over to the last of their group.

Sam. *Sam killed Richard Lomas so that he could*

scoop up the guesthouse from Evangeline and turn it into a thriving business that laundered, not washing, but money, maybe both!

Of all the motives she'd come up with, Roxy had to admit that this one seemed the most likely, except for the fact that Sam appeared as straight as an arrow. She forced herself to consider him though. She wondered how long Sam had been around. Was he really as much a part of the furniture as he looked? Or was he a relative stranger who had ingratiated himself for nefarious reasons?

Roxy watched the parade go by, feeling a little spaced-out and confused. Despite thinking in-depth about everyone, the situation didn't feel any clearer.

Her head pounded with all the twists and turns. Her brain couldn't hold all her thoughts, much like her clenched hand couldn't hold all the glitter. She could see the beautiful mix of purple and gold spilling through her fingers. What would she wish for?

She knew, of course, that glitter wouldn't *really* make anything happen. But it posed an interesting question . . . What *could* she wish for? What *did* she really want? If only she knew!

With a little jump, she shot her arm into the air and let go of the glitter. *I wish I knew what I wanted for my life! I wish I knew where I was going next!*

It seemed something of a non-wish, but it was the best she could come up with. At the very least, it was sincere. Drifting away above the heads of the crowd, the glitter caught the breeze and the gold and purple flecks dipped and swirled before fading to nothingness. Roxy watched it as it floated away.

As the group of friends ambled back to Evangeline's a couple of hours later, Roxy wondered about the idea of staying in New Orleans long term. She loved the music that seemed to seep from every corner of the city. She loved the bright shotgun houses that were painted just about every color under the sun—one hot pink, the next canary yellow, the next a deep forest green. She loved the food and wondered hopefully if it might bulk out her slight, childlike figure a little.

She loved . . . Well, it was hard to explain . . . But, she guessed, if she were being like Sage, she would have called it "the vibe." The place had a warm, wraparound feeling to it, like stepping into your favorite grandmother's kitchen, or at least what she imagined it would feel like if she had a favorite grandmother. Perhaps she did know what she wanted to do next after all . . .

As soon as they got back to the guesthouse, Evangeline was all smiles. Roxy realized it was the first time she'd seen her smile like that. She seemed lighter, happier.

"Everyone!" she said, clapping her hands at them in the hallway. "As y'all are here, I want to make an announcement. I've come to a big decision. First of all, I want to thank you for your offer to buy this old crumblin' place, Sam. I've known you since you were a child, cher, and your generosity has always shined. This ole lady is duly grateful."

On hearing this, Roxy immediately dismissed her earlier theory that Sam was a recent arrival and a fraud. If he was a cheat, he was deceiving people he had known for years. It seemed improbable.

Evangeline held her hand out for Louise to take. "But Louise and I have been talkin', and I've decided she is gonna be the new owner here."

Louise smiled a brave kind of smile and nodded like she was still trying to convince herself. "I know it's a bold move, but you only get one chance at life," she told the group. "I came here to start over, and that's what I'm going to do. I'm not going to be put off by what happened to Richard Lomas. It's a terrible tragedy, but I won't fall apart. You can rely on me, and I'll work like crazy to get Evangeline's back on its feet."

Evangeline nodded. "That's what I like to hear, cher."

"What will you do, Evangeline?" Sam asked. He looked tired but resigned.

"You'll have to find out, cher," Evangeline said with a wink and a sly smile.

Sam laughed. "Who knows what the next crazy chapter will be in Evangeline's book of life, huh?"

"You got that right, my boy."

"Congratulations, Louise! It is wonderful news. Don't forget, my bakery is at your service, night and day," Elijah said, taking Louise's hand. With a deep bow he planted a kiss on the back of it.

"Yes, congratulations," Sage said. "Let me know if you need the website updated."

Nat stared at Louise, mulishly. She looked threatening, but Roxy knew Nat well enough by now to know she was feeling very nervous. "Um, congratulations Louise," Nat mumbled. There was a pause. "Don't suppose you'll be keeping me on, will you?" she finally piped up, her voice tight and high.

"Of course, I will!" Louise said. "You might have to change up your clothing to match the new décor, but that's all."

"Right," said Nat, crossing her arms, but keeping her cool. "Thank you," she said, nodding.

"*Hello*!" A woman's voice carried through the lobby, her voice dripping with insincere gaiety. "How nice to find you all here. Have I interrupted something?"

They turned to the doorway.

"Mara Lomas!" Nat exclaimed. Mara smiled from ear to ear. "What are you doing here? We thought you were in police custody!"

Mara looked distinctly disheveled compared with the last time they had seen her. Her stilettos had been replaced by old running shoes. Her hair was straggly and pulled back in a messy bun. Her face was still a picture of fury, though. "The police have finally seen sense and accepted that I didn't murder my husband. Now I want to find out who did. I know that Richard was trying to cut a deal here before he was shot so it was probably one of you guys."

Roxy's eyes flickered down to Mara's hand—she was wearing her wedding ring. Roxy was sure she hadn't been wearing it the last time she saw her.

"What do you care?" Nat said. "You hated the guy. He was cheating on you. You didn't exactly sound like his greatest fan when you came over here before."

Mara strode up to Nat and grabbed her by the face, her hand under Nat's chin, her fingers pushing into her cheeks. "Don't you *dare* talk about me and my dead husband like that!"

"Get off me!" Nat said, gripping Mara's wrist and tearing the woman's hand from her face.

"You keep quiet if you can't tell me something helpful, do you hear?" Mara shouted. A tear fell down her cheek, and she wiped it away, furious. "Tell me, who killed my husband? Who?"

No one said anything.

"Tell me!" Mara screamed, her eyes popping.

"I'm sorry, cher," Evangeline said. "We don't have no idea what happened to . . ."

"It was one of you," said Mara, narrowing her eyes. She picked up a letter knife from the hallway table and pointed it at each of the folks assembled in front of her. "I'm sure of it. Now you're all covering for each other. I know it. I do. I'm 100% certain."

Roxy's heart was beating faster than usual. It always did when someone yelled or got mad (or was waving a knife at her.)

"No one knows who killed Richard," Sam said softly. "We want to know, too, but none of us are investigators."

"Maybe not. I bet one of you is a murderer though," said Mara, bitterness lacing her voice.

"Detective Johnson is still investigating," Elijah said. "I'm sure he'll find out who is responsible in the end."

"Him!" Mara said. She snorted. "He likes to play the big shot. He has traumatized me all over again. *Helping them with their inquiries.* That's no way to treat a grieving widow, is it?"

"No, it isn't," Sam agreed. His deep voice could be wonderfully soothing. "He's not the gentlest guy in town, but he's a good detective. He simply wants to find out what happened to your husband, that's all."

It seemed that Sam's compassion took all the wind out of Mara's sails. "Well," she said, dropping the letter knife. "I'll be back, but don't think any of you are off the hook. I *will* find out who did this. And they *will* be sorry."

She left, a little wobbly on her feet as she strode away, but thanks to her running shoes, she negotiated the cobblestones a little easier than she had last time.

As she watched Mara leave, Roxy was almost sure that what she'd just witnessed couldn't have been a performance. Mara had *not* killed Richard Lomas. Roxy was certain. She would have put money on it. So, if it wasn't her, *who was it*?

CHAPTER TWENTY-SIX

THAT NIGHT, ROXY couldn't sleep. Now, the idea was really dawning on her that she may well be sleeping under the same roof as a murderer. Or at the very least, associating with one. She hated the thought and her brain buzzed with theories until she got a headache.

She opened her eyes and stared at the ceiling, trying to shut her mind down so she could drift off to sleep. It wasn't working. Nefertiti was curled up next to her. She was purring so loudly she sounded like some sort of engine. Roxy absentmindedly pushed her fingertips through Nefertiti's fur as her mind did all sorts of gymnastics she couldn't control.

It was then that she heard a bloodcurdling

scream. It came from the room below her. Roxy sat bolt upright, her heart racing. "Oh, my gosh!"

Roxy scrambled out of bed and rushed from the room. Then she realized she could be in danger and didn't have a weapon. She looked around. What could she use? Her eyes fell upon a large candlestick, and she rushed to snatch it up. She doubted she'd have the strength to swing it around or cause some real damage if it came to it, but it was better than nothing.

She rushed down the stairs in bare feet and came across Louise, who was outside her room, clutching her chest, hyperventilating.

"Oh, my goodness, what happened?!" Roxy asked. "Are you okay?"

Louise gulped and tried to catch a breath. "I don't . . . I don't know! Someone was in my bedroom!" Her voice was slurred, and Roxy caught the scent of whiskey heavy on her breath.

"What? Who?"

"I don't know!" Louise squeaked. "It was dark. I couldn't see. I think he thought I was asleep, but then I gave him such a fright when I got up that he jumped out of the window. I tried to look down the street but I couldn't make him out—he was wearing all black and a ski mask." She leaned against the doorframe, still breathing heavily.

Roxy puffed out a breath. "This is getting serious now, Louise."

"Right?" Louise let out another big breath. "Oh, Roxy," she said. "I have to tell you."

"What? What do you have to tell me?"

Louise looked around, as though someone might be lurking in the stairway. "Come into my room. I want to show you something," she hissed.

Louise snapped on the light, and Roxy saw that her eyes were bloodshot. The path she made toward the bed was winding and wobbly.

"I've done something *terrible,*" Louise said, "and I don't know how to get myself out of it." She sat at the head of her bed, rummaging in her nightstand drawer. "I don't know if it's connected to what happened tonight. Maybe."

"What? What have you done, Louise?"

Louise patted the bed, and Roxy sat down. The older woman took yet another deep breath, then reached further into the nightstand drawer. She pulled out a phone. She put it on the bed and removed her hands quickly as though she might catch a horrible disease from it.

"Your phone," Roxy said, waiting for an explanation.

"No," said Louise, her voice cracking. "Not *my* phone." She whispered, "Richard Lomas' phone!"

Roxy gasped. "How did you get that?!" Her voice was loud with surprise.

"Shhhh!" Louise said furiously. "Oh, gosh." She shook her head, and then covered her eyes with her hand. "I made a *huge* mistake."

Roxy's heart started thumping so violently she could feel it in her temples.

"When I found him . . . I . . . I don't really know what happened. I saw his phone on the ground, near his hand. His cold, dead, outstretched hand." Louise was nearly in tears. "He had a bunch of flowers with him, too. I don't know why. I just took them both. I threw away the flowers, but I slipped the phone into my pocket. I don't know what I was thinking. I was just . . . in shock, I guess."

"Oh."

"And then I didn't tell Detective Johnson because I didn't know how, and every hour since then I've resolved to, but still I haven't. It's just got harder and harder, and now we're here . . . I can't possibly tell him after all this time. I look so guilty. Oh help, what have I done?!" Louise leaned over and took both of Roxy's hands in hers, her eyes wide, imploring Roxy to understand.

Roxy shook her head. The situation was a real mess.

"I considered not telling him at all," said Louise. "But the thing is . . . there's *evidence* on this phone."

"Really?" Roxy said sitting up straight. "What kind of evidence?"

"Take the phone yourself and read the text messages," said Louise. "We're going to *have* to turn it in. It might make all the difference in the investigation."

Roxy was hesitant to pick up the phone. She'd already noticed that Louise was using the word "we," essentially drawing Roxy into her predicament, but she was too curious about what was on the phone to let that stop her. She wasn't about to allow the chance of finding evidence pass her by because she felt a little uncertain.

Roxy picked up the phone.

"One particular thread of messages is of note," Louise said. She looked away and up at the ceiling of her room.

Roxy tapped the phone and there, the first contact was *Elijah Walder.* She let out a little gasp. "Elijah? As in Elijah, Elijah?"

"You got it," Louise said.

Roxy clicked into the conversation and immediately scrolled up to the top, to see it all in chronological order. It was full of messages that showed Richard Lomas and Elijah had been in constant contact for a period of time.

I've sent you the proposal by email.

It was a message from Lomas to Elijah read. Elijah had responded.

When are you next in the area?

"What does it mean, do you think?" Roxy wondered out loud to Louise. "The proposal? Obviously, they were doing some kind of business together, but what? Do you think Elijah was involved in trying to get Evangeline to sell the guesthouse?" Her mind turned over, thinking back over all the times she'd been around the baker. She didn't remember ever seeing him try to influence Evangeline's decision or even discuss the deal with her.

"No," Louise said. "Keep scrolling."

"He was thinking of selling the bakery?" said Roxy as she read.

"Yes. But then things got a little hairy."

Roxy read on. Elijah had written:

That price is an insult. This is my family business. It was passed down from my grandfather. I would expect much better compensation.

Lomas had written back:

I'm not interested in your business. Not even in the building. Only the land upon which the business and building are situated.

Elijah had responded furiously:

NO DEAL.

The last message in the thread was one from Lomas:

We'll see about that. I have my ways and means. You having a little tantrum won't stop me.

CHAPTER TWENTY-SEVEN

ROXY READ THE text messages three times before she handed the phone back to Louise. "So . . . do you think it was Elijah who snuck into your room just now? Do you think he was going to hurt you?"

"Yes . . . no . . ." Louise said, looking a little lost. She put her hands up to her face. "Oh, I just don't know."

A tense, pregnant silence stretched out between them as they both considered what might have happened.

"Well, you'll have to hand this cell phone into Detective Johnson," Roxy said. "But . . . let's wait a bit, a few more hours won't make any difference now. You just focus on how you're going to transform this place. You've had enough trauma and drama as it is. I'm going to do some investigating of my own. We'll hand the cell phone in after that."

Back in her room, there was no chance now that Roxy would get any sleep. She lay on the bed for a while, tossing and turning, but eventually gave up. She rose and opened her linen curtains. The sky was just beginning to edge out of darkness.

She wished she had someone to talk to, someone to bounce her ideas off. She didn't want to trouble Louise any more—she'd been through enough already. Besides, even with this information on Elijah, she couldn't entirely rule Louise out as a suspect. Neither could she rule out Nat or Evangeline. Sam would have made a good confidante, she was sure, but she was still a little suspicious of him too. Plus, she had to admit to herself, she had a crush on him that didn't help her keep a clear head. What about Sage?

Sage was usually up at dawn to perform her rituals, "Before the rest of the world gets up and clogs the energy space with their vibes," she had told Roxy. She was busy with programming and tarot readings during the day, but in the serenity of the early morning, she was alone and available.

Before Roxy's mind was made up, her body got into gear. She rushed over to her wardrobe and picked out some jeans, a shirt, and a cardigan. "Bye,

Nef," she said as she slipped her sneakers on. "See you later, lovely girl."

She crept down the stairs, wincing at every creak, and let herself out of the front door into the cold morning air. She looked over at Elijah's bakery and gave a little involuntary shiver. She went out onto the cobblestones and looked back at Evangeline's. Below her own rickety balcony was Louise's room. Roxy looked at the open window and saw the thick old-fashioned drainpipe next to it. That, and the ledges that were built between the floors as part of the architectural style meant that it would be easy for someone to climb up or down.

Roxy pulled her cardigan around her to keep herself protected from the cold air then headed out of the cobbled alleyway and onto the street.

A black car pulled up to the curb next to her. Johnson stepped out of it, his face creased with barely concealed rage as usual. Roxy gulped. She had every intention of telling Johnson about the phone, but not now. Now, she wanted to avoid him.

"You," he said.

Roxy tried to find a smile. "Good morning, Detective Johnson."

He curled his lip. "A little birdy tells me you're sneaking around, doing *detective work.*"

Roxy's heart stopped.

He edged up horribly close to her. "Listen up,

lady. I'm the detective, you're just a guest in our city. Stay in your lane, okay?" He stepped back a pace. "And I sincerely hope you're not out here at this early hour doing any *investigating.*"

"Oh, no," Roxy lied. "I'm going to see Sage, for . . . some spiritual help. I'm not feeling so good."

"You'll be feeling a whole lot worse if you keep meddling," he said. He waved his hand, dismissively. "Keep moving. Go on, go."

Roxy scurried across the road, then headed up a stairway around the side of a store and up to Sage's apartment that was located on top. She looked down at the street to see Johnson staring up at her. An ice-cold shiver ran through her, and she quickly turned away. She had wanted to see if he was going into the guesthouse, but she couldn't bear to watch. Anyway, she suspected he would remain there staring at her until she was out of his sight.

Roxy took a deep breath and knocked on Sage's door. As she waited for Sage to answer, Roxy wondered if she was doing the right thing.

"A visitor through the midst of esoteric time," Roxy heard Sage say through the door.

It opened, and Sage stood before her, looking quite different from normal. Her long mermaid hair was gone, a short afro in its place. She had on soft white robes but was without her characteristic jewelry. Her brown eyes seemed to penetrate deep into

Roxy's soul, however. She didn't break into her usual warm smile. She didn't even speak further. She just nodded and stepped to the side to let Roxy through.

"Oh, um, thanks," Roxy said in a quiet voice, then berated herself for speaking at all. There was an atmosphere between them, a different ambiance from usual, but Roxy couldn't quite put her finger on what it was or why it was there.

Sage led her through the plain, ordinary hallway, with its white walls and wooden floor, and into a back room. Roxy gasped. It was like stepping into another world.

CHAPTER TWENTY-EIGHT

THE ROOM WAS draped with silk hangings, in rich shades of orange and crimson and deep pink, which should have clashed, but somehow looked wonderful together. The smell of incense hung thick and sweet in the air, as white smoke unfurled in a graceful dance above four incense burners placed in each corner. Three white candles were burning in large glass jars, their flames flickering. They sat atop a white-clothed table in the center of the room. A clear bowl full of water sat in front of them. Cushions were laid out on the dark wooden floor, orange and deep red and pink like the drapes, and a deck of tarot cards were spread in an elaborate formation in front of them. The whole effect was mesmerizing.

"Wow," Roxy said under her breath.

Sage sat on a crimson cushion and gestured for Roxy to do the same. When she turned to look at her, her eyes were bright. "It is no coincidence you have come here now, at this time. This is no ordinary visit. I can feel the difference. Spirit has carried you here."

Roxy didn't quite know what to say so she looked down at her lap, mumbling hesitantly, her gaze flickering up to Sage's face and down to her lap again. "Well . . . I came here to run something by you. Something about the murder. Some information I've found out." Sage simply nodded.

Roxy decided to face Sage squarely and proceeded to tell her everything that Louise had told her. She also told Sage about the text messages between Lomas and Elijah. The tall African American woman listened intently. Once Roxy was done, Sage stared at the candles. She closed her eyes, and took a deep breath, exhaling with a long outward breath. She stayed still for such a long time that Roxy wondered if she had fallen asleep.

Roxy cast her eyes over the tarot cards on the floor. She still didn't know if she believed in them or not, but surely trying them out couldn't hurt.

Sage opened her eyes. "Let us consult the cards," she said.

Roxy flinched, wondering if it was a coincidence, or if Sage was reading her mind. "That's just what I was thinking!"

Sage raised an eyebrow. She scooped up all the tarot cards and began to shuffle them. First, she did so in her hand then she placed the deck on the floor face down. She pushed the deck over and spread the cards out before moving them around the floor until they were well mixed.

"Right," Sage said, rocking back on her heels. "Ask your question."

Roxy tried to get into a positive mindset and not let doubt take over. "Okay . . . How is Elijah involved in the murder of Richard Lomas?"

"Point to three cards."

Roxy did as she was told and Sage laid the three cards in a row face down. "Ready?" she said.

Roxy gulped, not sure that she was. The seriousness of the situation was beginning to kick in. She was in a strange city, had placed herself in the middle of a murder investigation, and here she was using tarot cards to check her suspicions. The whole thing was just so, so far out of her normal experience, and yet, here she was. It was happening. It was real. "Yes," she said.

"This card represents the past," Sage said. She turned the first card over. "The Seven of Swords." There was a picture of a man carrying knives in his arms, sneaking away, as if he were stealing them.

"Deception," said Sage. "Someone is trying to get away with something, undetected." She rolled her eyes and laughed. "Really, universe? You don't say!" She immediately got serious again. "Someone has false motives and has been pursuing an agenda of their own. Someone has been keeping secrets and deceiving others."

Roxy's heart beat a little faster. Maybe these cards really *did* work! Were they talking about Elijah? It seemed the tarot cards were just as ready to condemn him as his text messages.

"Right, the next card represents the present," Sage said. She flipped it over and raised her eyebrows. "Ace of Swords," she said, as if in a trance. "Communication needs to be clarified. Persevere in your quest for an answer even if it is not the one you wish for."

Roxy's eyes popped. She *didn't* like the idea of Elijah being the killer. After all, he was part of the little group she had become quite attached to. He made the loveliest beignets. He seemed kind and, though a little outlandish, good-hearted. Sam and Elijah were great friends and excellent music partners, but what was really known about him?

"Now for the final card," Sage said. "This determines the future." She flipped it over. "Death."

Roxy gasped. "Another murder?"

"No," said Sage. "It means total transformation.

The complete and dramatic end of something. Starting over."

Roxy let out a deep breath and looked at Sage. "So . . . do you think this means Elijah is the killer?"

Sage pursed her lips together. "It's impossible to tell, honey. Some people say you can get yes and no answers from the cards, but that's overly simplistic. They're much more complex and layered than that. You have to mix the meanings in with your intuition. What's your gut telling you?"

Roxy paused. "I don't know," she said. She had all sorts of feelings and impressions swirling around, but any time she tried to fix her mind on Elijah being the murderer, another possibility popped up. Nat. Mara. Evangeline. It was impossible to know. "I just don't know." She peered at Sage, who was now staring intently at the incense as it swirled and danced up to the ceiling. She wondered just how much Sage knew—how much secret knowledge her spiritual powers truly afforded her. "Do *you* know?"

"I wish I did," said Sage. "Life is full of mysteries. I spend my time on this earth trying to decode them, but some are complex. They only reveal themselves when they desire it."

"Well, I hope they desire it real soon," Roxy said, thinking about the intruder Louise found in her room, "before someone else gets hurt."

Sage nodded. "I'll put a protection spell over

the guesthouse to keep y'all safe. While that can help, it depends on the forces at play, and right now there are some real strong ones out there. I can feel them, dark ones, greedy ones, ready to harm for their own benefit."

Roxy felt a little panicked. "So what can we do?"

"Work fast," said Sage. "My role is to liaise with the spiritual forces present. I'll work with them as much as I can to bring justice, but we need feet on the ground. Practical work. Get out there and find the truth."

Roxy breathed. "I'll certainly try."

Sage smiled for the first time that morning. She reached out and squeezed Roxy's hand. "The spirits are on your side, sweetheart."

CHAPTER TWENTY-NINE

AS ROXY LEFT Sage's magical, mystical apartment, her mind went back to that first wonderfully cozy evening when they all holed up in Evangeline's dining room, eating spicy Creole food and listening to Elijah and Sam as they filled the place with the sounds of jazz.

Sam and Elijah seemed so close. They were truly in sync that night. Sure, they had performed some set pieces, but they had jammed together afterward, and it had flowed as easily as the wine.

If Elijah were the killer, as Roxy was grudgingly beginning to admit may be the case, surely Sam would be devastated. They were like brothers.

She meandered back toward the cobbled street where Evangeline's stood and paused for a moment.

She looked at the bakery to her left and Evangeline's to the right. The short distance between them had once seemed so quaint and intimate. Now the distance felt sinister, a huge black shadowy presence between them, one that possibly divided a murderer from his prey. Roxy shivered involuntarily, not from the cold, but from the mental image of Elijah sneaking out in the dead of night and climbing the pipes to Louise's room.

At that moment, Nat came out of the front door with a rug and began to shake it out. She looked up and jumped when she saw Roxy. "Blooming heck, Rox," she said. "You gave me one heck of a fright. What are you doing out and about so early?" Her face creased into a frown.

"Oh . . ." Roxy stared at Nat and wished she could explain. Everything was jumbled and muddled in her head, and it was starting to give her a headache. "I went to see Sage."

"Oh right." Nat went back to shaking out the rug, banging it against the railings and sending clouds of dust flying everywhere. She gave a happy smile. "So, Louise is taking over the guesthouse, and I get to stay on. Isn't that great?"

"Yep," Roxy said.

"Will you stay?"

"I . . . I don't know yet." Roxy was wary as she spoke to Nat. She didn't feel free to relax and chat normally. Anyone could be the killer. A thought popped into her head. "Do you know where I'd be able to find Sam?"

"He'll be at his laundry," Nat said. A teasing smile played at the corner of her lips. "Why?"

Roxy tried very hard not to blush. "I wanted to ask him . . ." There was a mischievous glint in Nat's eyes, so Roxy quickly made something up. "I wanted to ask him if he'd seen my . . . my . . . I think I left some money in one of my dress pockets. I want to see if I can rescue it before it gets put through the wash."

"Okay, if you say so," Nat said with a grin. "Well, the laundry isn't too far away. A couple of blocks. Go out of the front entrance, turn left, and walk on until you get to 24th Street. Take another left, and it's down there a couple of minutes. Sam's Laundry. You can't miss it."

Roxy took off immediately, keen to get away from Nat but also because she didn't want to think too much about her decision to speak to Sam about what she knew.

The directions were easy to follow, and before long she was standing on the steps of the laundry. She could see clothing and linens tumbling inside the machines.

She entered and a little bell tinkled. The temperature was several degrees higher inside the laundry, a pleasing contrast to the cool outside.

"Hello," she said. Sam was behind the front desk attending to some paperwork. He didn't move. Individually, each of the machines made only gentle whirring noises, but together they created a distinct thrum, and she realized she'd have to raise her voice to make herself heard. "Hello!" Sam looked up this time, and a huge smile spread across his face. Roxy felt heat rising to her cheeks, and she had to look at the floor for a moment.

"Hi, Roxy. What a great surprise!" he said, standing up and showing his Southern manners.

"Hi, Sam." Roxy cleared her throat, reminding herself that she was here on a serious mission. There was no time to be embarrassed or to pay attention to how her legs felt. It was as though they were turning to jelly.

"To what do I owe the pleasure of this visit?" he asked. He brought out a chair from behind the counter and placed it in front of her. "Please, take a seat."

"Thank you." Roxy sat down, and taking his cue from her, he did, too. She forced herself to look up into his dreamy blue eyes. "This isn't a pleasure visit, I'm afraid."

Sam didn't blink. "That's a shame."

"I'm going to be 100% straight with you," said Roxy.

"Good! It's about time." A smile played at the corner of his lips.

"What?"

"Oh, come on. We both . . ." he trailed off. Roxy was utterly bewildered.

A look of panic sprung into Sam's eyes. "Erm . . . I mean to say, you know . . . erm . . . you'll be staying on at the guesthouse, won't you?" He began to talk very fast. "I mean, you keep saying you don't know, you don't know, but I think we both know you will."

"Oh," Roxy said. "Well, yeah, I think I will. For a while anyway." She laughed awkwardly. "You got me there, skipper." What was she saying? *Skipper?*

He looked immensely relieved. "New Orleans is like that. Once it gets its hooks into you, it doesn't want to give you back. I grew up here, of course. I tried going away to college, but I came straight back after I graduated and opened my first business. My father was furious. He wanted me to go into investment banking in New York."

They settled into a comfortable silence. The whir of the machines went on. Roxy liked the sound. The moment felt cozy and intimate, but she knew she had to broach the subject of Elijah sooner or later. She opened her mouth.

"Sam, I . . ."

"Roxy, I . . ."

They spoke at the same time. They laughed.

"Go on," he said. His eyes were sparkling. Roxy got the distinct feeling that he thought she was going to ask him on a date. In truth, she didn't want the moment to end. She felt this pleasant, electric tension between them, but she had no plans to invite him out. She just didn't do that kind of thing.

Instead, she took a deep breath. "I have reason to believe that Elijah might have been involved in Richard Lomas' murder."

CHAPTER THIRTY

SAM'S OPEN, EXPECTANT expression changed immediately. It crumpled into a deep, concerned frown.

"What?" he breathed. "No."

"I'm so sorry. I know you won't want to believe that, but . . . there's a lot of evidence that points in that direction." Roxy explained about the phone, and the break-in, and the conversations that had been going on between Elijah and Richard.

Sam started pushing paperwork around unnecessarily. He shuffled his papers and stacked them. Then he unstacked them again. Roxy doubted he even registered what he was doing.

"Well, I think you're wrong," he said, his voice hard. He frowned and rubbed the back of his neck.

Roxy felt tension—now the utterly wrong kind of tension—course through her body. "I wish I were, Sam, but . . ."

"But what?" he said. "Honestly, Roxy, I think you should let this go. Detective Johnson is . . ."

Suddenly Roxy felt quite angry. "Detective Johnson is *what*?" she interrupted, surprising herself with the steel in her voice. "An idiot, if you ask me."

"So you know better than him about investigating, do you?"

"You've sure changed your tune!" Roxy snapped. "You said he might be corrupt."

"Well, maybe," Sam said. "But the alternative isn't for us to go around playing cop."

"Playing cop?!" Roxy said. "Excuse me for caring. I'm trying to ensure Evangeline isn't the subject of a miscarriage of justice!"

Sam leaned back in his chair and tapped his fingers on the desk in irritation. "Okay, let's say Johnson is corrupt and will pin the murder on whoever he wants. You think you can stand up to him and the whole police department?"

"Well, no, but . . ." Roxy floundered.

"Look, Roxy, you're not from this town," Sam said. His voice was a little kinder now. " You don't know what goes on behind the scenes."

Roxy felt a horrible knot in her stomach. "I'm just trying to . . ."

"Well, don't," Sam said. "Don't try. I know you mean well, but you're a visitor to this city, a tourist. Let the police sort it out. If Evangeline does get charged with Lomas' murder, I'll get the best lawyers on the case. *That's* what's going to help. Not this. Not you."

Roxy swallowed, tears threatened to well, but she held her head high. "I think you're only saying this because you don't want to face the fact that Elijah might have done it."

Sam shook his head. "Louise needs to hand in that phone and prepare herself for the consequences. She could go to jail for keeping it. It's theft at best. Obstructing the course of justice at worst."

"But she was in shock!"

"Do you think Johnson will give a rat's behind about shock?"

"No, but . . ."

"This is not cool," he said. "Not cool at all. Louise has got herself in too deep. And now you're doing the same. This is going to blow up in your faces. Johnson might even put *you* in jail for knowing about the phone and doing nothing about it."

Roxy had been so wrapped up in her investigation, she hadn't even thought of that. His words were like a bucket of ice water dumped over her head. "He wouldn't," she said, but her voice wobbled. She imagined herself in jail with a bunch of tough women. From a steady job with a steady boyfriend, renting a nice apartment with savings in the bank . . . to that? Maybe this move had been a terrible idea after all. Maybe she was crazy even being in New Orleans, let alone getting herself mixed up in all of this. "Johnson wouldn't be that cruel," she said, although she suspected that he would.

"Look, Roxy, I don't mean to be harsh, but you have to be realistic. Both you and Louise have come into town and gotten yourselves wrapped up in a serious issue, an issue that could have big implications. Life-changing implications. I know New Orleans is a mystical place, but don't get caught up in the hype of Mardi Gras and Sage's spiritualism and think that magic will fix this. It won't. Despite the wonder of this city, it isn't immune from the harsher aspects of life. It won't give you a happy-ever-after ending just because. Reality is dirty and gritty and messy here, just like everywhere else."

Roxy didn't know what to say. She felt heavy all over. Her limbs were like lead. "Right," she said, still trying to inject a little sass into her voice.

Sam sighed. "I'm not trying to be unpleasant,

Roxy," he said, his voice softening again. "I just want you to be realistic."

Now, Roxy felt patronized. She shot him a glare. "You just don't want to consider that Elijah might be a murderer," she repeated.

"I don't know about that." Sam shook his head. "I certainly don't think he is, but maybe I'm wrong. I hope not. But the truth will out. The police will find out who did it. It won't be tourists solving this, digging around like they're on a murder mystery weekend."

"Stop calling me a tourist!" Roxy snapped.

"But that's what you *are,*" he said softly. "You've only been here a few days. You don't really know New Orleans yet. She's a mysterious, unpredictable old girl."

Roxy, her eyes gleaming furiously, stood. "I'm going back to Evangeline's. I'll take my washing, if you don't mind."

"Don't you want me to drive it over? I have laundry for the others, too."

"I'll take it all," Roxy said icily.

"You sure? It's a big pile."

"Fine with me."

"Come on, don't be like that. I'll take you."

"No, thank you."

Sam sighed and went into the back room. He came out with several parcels of washing, all wrapped up with paper and string. "Here you go." He put them on his table.

Roxy stacked them and picked them up carefully. She just about managed to carry them all and started forward, peering over the top. One parcel fell off, but Sam caught it and popped it back on. "Look," he said, when they were so close she could smell the deep, alluring musk of his aftershave. "I didn't mean to make you feel bad. I just . . ."

Roxy put on a big smile. It was like a weapon. "You didn't make me feel bad. You made me feel more certain," she said, making for the door. "Bye, Sam."

CHAPTER THIRTY-ONE

"WE'RE PULLING OUT all the stops tonight!" Evangeline said. "Louise is taking over my business. We're celebrating!" Evangeline's eyes were bright, but her voice was brittle and Roxy suspected that despite her brave face, Evangeline wasn't as happy as she seemed. Old age was forcing her to hand her guesthouse over, and Roxy knew that Evangeline would be feeling burning shame and grief at losing her independence, her livelihood, and her beloved building.

"Come and help in the kitchen," Nat had said, catching Roxy as she came back from her angry visit to the laundry. "We're cooking up a storm!"

Roxy was still piled high with parcels and decided to take them to her room. She'd distribute them later. Nefertiti lazily looked up when she came in. Roxy tickled the cat under her chin as she lay curled up in a chair before rushing down the stairs to help. She felt so mixed up and confused that she thought a good cooking session with Nat and Evangeline, both fierce, no-nonsense women, would make her feel better.

The warm aroma of Creole spices drifted from the kitchen around the ground floor and up the stairs, immediately making Roxy feel at home again. *Forget Sam, and forget the murder investigation for now.*

As soon as Roxy stepped into the kitchen, which was thick with steam and spice, Evangeline called out, "It's beignets or nothing for breakfast, cher. This kitchen's occupied all day."

"I came to help," Roxy said. She'd gotten up so early, it was hard to believe that it wasn't yet ten o'clock.

"Aha!" Evangeline said. "Another pair of hands. Suits me."

Nat grinned and held out the plate of beignets to Roxy. "And you can't eat as you go, so have your fill now."

Roxy took one gratefully. Despite her fast metabolism, she was sure she'd get to be the size of a house if she lived in New Orleans permanently. She took a bite. "So what are we making?"

"A Creole feast!" Nat said excitedly, taking a pan from a cupboard and whirling it around.

"Stop that, or you'll put someone's eye out!" Evangeline snapped. She was chopping copious amounts of onion and garlic at lightning speed. "Let me tell you what we're making, cher: a little turtle soup to start, then a crawfish pie . . ."

"My *absolute* favorite," Nat said.

"Next, our main dish." Evangeline swelled with pride. "Barbecued shrimp with Eggs Hussarde, collard greens, smothered okra, potato casserole on the side, and a jalapeño shrimp cornbread."

"In little ramekins," Nat added happily. "They look *so* cute."

"Wow," said Roxy. "That sounds like quite a spread."

"You betcha, cher," Evangeline said. "It's a mashup of my grandmomma's classics. You won't find that combination anywhere else, not in New Orleans, not in the whole world."

"I can believe that," Roxy said. She felt her mood lift.

"And to finish, New Orleans bread pudding with whiskey sauce," said Nat. She was practically bouncing around the kitchen. Roxy guessed her mood was partly to do with the feast, but mostly because she wasn't facing the threat of deportation any longer.

"Now, as a clever girl, you'll already have guessed that we'll be on our feet all darn day," Evangeline said. "And there's plenty to do. Want to chop a mountain of onions?" Roxy wrinkled her nose.

"Well then, you know how to purge crawfish?"

Roxy giggled. "Nope. Absolutely not."

"I could do it at four years old," Evangeline said. "Every good N'awlins girl can. Nat, show her."

Nat took Roxy by the hand and dragged her into a small back room that had an outside door. She pointed at a large bucket of squirming crawfish. "I hope you're not squeamish!" she said.

Roxy hadn't seen crawfish before. She looked at their shiny black shells and long red pincers. They waved at her, and she did, in all honesty, feel a little nervous of them, but she wouldn't let on to Nat. She pasted a big smile on her face. "I'm ready."

"Good. You have to purge to get all the mud out of them," Nat said, getting out a big basin. "Right, tip all the crawfish in there."

Roxy did so.

"Next we pour a bunch of salt over them." Nat grabbed a bag of salt from the side and sprinkled liberally. "Then hot water. Fill up that jug there." Roxy filled the jug with hot water. "Go ahead, pour it in the bucket." Roxy poured, and the water began to turn brown.

"Ew," Nat said. "See all that muck?" She kneeled and began to stir the crawfish around the basin with a metal spoon. The crawfish squirmed and splashed in the water. Nat looked up at Roxy and grinned. "New Orleans doesn't look so glamorous now, huh?"

Roxy laughed.

Nat poked around with the spoon. "We have to fish out any dead ones. Evangeline will go bananas if they end up in the pot. Oh, look, there's one," she said, scooping it out. She flicked it in the trash. "Now we gotta drain them."

Soon they were back in the kitchen over a boiling pot of water. Nat added garlic powder, cayenne pepper, sticks of butter, oranges, lemons, and a whole load of powder called "Crab Boil."

Evangeline stood with her arms folded, casting a watchful eye over their progress. "Let that cook a little."

Roxy stood holding the large strainer of wriggling crawfish, as Evangeline poured some hot sauce into the bubbling mix.

"You're gonna burn our mouths!" Nat protested.

Roxy coughed as the mixture sent its spicy steam into her face.

Evangeline laughed at her. "A little spice is good for the soul, cher. Now tip in them crawfish, and let's get this pot goin'."

CHAPTER THIRTY-TWO

ALL DAY THEY cooked. Roxy grabbed a grilled cheese sandwich for lunch, and the time flew by as she thoroughly enjoyed herself. Before long, the day turned into evening, and most everything was ready.

"Now you two, go put on your glad-rags while I finish up here," said Evangeline.

Roxy headed upstairs and fed Nefertiti. She couldn't wait to have a hot shower, but before she did, she flopped down on the bed and kicked off her shoes. Her feet were aching, her whole body was aching.

"Oh, Nef-nef," she said, sighing happily. "Do you really think New Orleans will become our home?" Nefertiti was far too interested in her bowl of food to reply.

Roxy's earlier rush of anger toward Sam had blown itself out. All that chopping, stirring, boiling, and cleaning had purged her of it. She could even concede that he was probably right. She should just enjoy her time here and leave the investigating to the pros. If Evangeline wound up in court, of *course* Sam would pay for the best lawyers and get her off. Why had Roxy ever felt any of this was her responsibility? She looked back on it all and felt a little embarrassed. It was as if she had been a child playing detective.

It had felt like an adventure, but Sam was right. Roxy wasn't an investigator. She was a call-center operator. Actually, she wasn't even *that* anymore. As he said, she was a tourist, just a visitor passing through.

Roxy felt her mood about to take a nosedive. Her mind started to fill with the same old anxieties and questions about where she would go, what she would do, and how she would survive.

"Nope," she said out loud. "Not today."

The evening was going to be wonderful. They would feast, Sam and Elijah would play their wonderful jazz music, and the whole world would come to a standstill for a while. They couldn't escape reality completely, but they could lock it out of the guesthouse for a few hours.

Roxy decided to look on the bright side. She took a long hot shower and padded around the room in her slippers, humming happy tunes to keep her spirits up. She managed to remember one from the parade that they'd pumped out of the speakers over and over again, and it made her feel cheerful and relaxed.

She planned her evening. She would put on a little makeup and some jewelry and if she paired that with one of her freshly laundered dresses, she might feel like a million bucks. Roxy walked over to the chair where she had left the bundles she'd brought back from Sam's. She carried them to the bed and immediately noticed she had a problem.

The outsides of the parcels weren't labeled with names, but rather with numbers. So whose was whose? Roxy couldn't tell. She pondered for a moment. There was nothing for it. She'd have to open each parcel to find out to whom it belonged.

Roxy slipped the string that bound the bundles to the side, and opened them one by one, sifting through the clothes deliberately. It wouldn't do to mix them up. One parcel contained a pair of pants and as Roxy picked it up, she felt something hard and smooth and flat in the pocket. Slipping her fingers inside, she pulled out a laminated card. Her heart started thumping.

No way. It couldn't be possible. Roxy stared at the card.

"Oh, my goodness," she said. The world was spinning. "Oh, my gosh."

As Roxy sashayed down the stairs, she felt rather glamorous. She was wearing her red dress and her big, gold, hoop earrings while on her feet were espadrilles, their red straps crisscrossing her ankles and up her slim legs. She didn't normally go in for standout pizazz, she was modest in her choice of clothing, more of a wallflower, but tonight she felt a sense of confidence she'd never felt before. Her uncertainty and confusion were gone; determination burned deep in her soul.

"Oh wow, you look gorgeous!" Nat said as they met in the hallway.

Nat wore her regular clothes, only with a bit more bling; on her feet were shiny bottle-green boots with sparkly laces. "*Love* your boots," Roxy said.

Nat grinned. "Thanks! They're my favorites." She wrinkled her nose and smiled.

Roxy gasped as she walked into the dining

room. It had been completely transformed since breakfast. One long, grand dining table covered with huge, heavy, white tablecloths bisected the room. There was so much silver, china, and crystal that Roxy wasn't sure how the table legs didn't buckle. White plates lay on gold placemats, and down the center sat candelabras, white candles flickering. Between the candelabras were silver platters upon which the food they were about to feast on lay under silver covers.

"This looks amazing!" Roxy said.

It smelled heavenly, too, that very specific New Orleans smell of deep, rich spices, meat, seafood, and baked bread, all rolled into one.

Sage had already arrived. Even though she was a vegetarian and the feast most decidedly was not, Sage would not miss it for anything. She wore a long flowing dress in a deep-sea blue. It was covered in lace and had draping sleeves and gorgeous little blue beaded details. Her natural hair shone with bouncy coils, and a wreath of blue flowers was woven into them. She smiled serenely at Roxy.

"You look . . ." Roxy was practically speechless. "You look . . . like a sea goddess!"

Sage laughed in such a deep, throaty way that Roxy felt the whole room warm up. "What a lovely thing to say!"

Soon everyone else arrived—Sam in a regular

black tuxedo, Elijah in an *ir*regular tuxedo, one with a loud orange African print. Louise wore a tight, bright yellow dress that accentuated her ample curves, and Evangeline, a pretty floral frock.

Nat looked around at them all and laughed, "Wow, we make quite a picture!"

"I'll say!" added Roxy. She and Sam shared a warm look over the table, letting each other know that they weren't still mad with each other.

"Come on, people, this ain't some fashion show!" Evangeline said. "Let's eat!"

CHAPTER THIRTY-THREE

THE MURDER, THE guesthouse handover, and the drama were all forgotten as they sank into the heartiest cuisine New Orleans had to offer. Plenty of wine washed it all down, and laughter echoed around the dining room.

After a long day, Roxy was hungry and eager to try everything but was a little wary of the soup. It was the first time she'd eaten turtle. Evangeline saw her clutching her spoon as she looked down at her bowl nervously.

"There are seven kinds of meat on a turtle, cher," Evangeline said. "Some folk say that it tastes of turkey, fish, veal, or pork, dependin' on the part you get. Nat and me, we take out the fish parts and leave the rest. That's how I learned it from my grandmomma. Give it a taste and see if it isn't one of the best darn things you ever did eat."

Roxy forced a smile. It did *smell* delicious, which made tasting it a little easier. "Here's goes," she said. She sipped a little off her spoon. "Ooh, it *does* taste like pork! It's lovely!"

Evangeline nodded proudly, "You bet, cher."

Next, they had crawfish pie, Nat's favorite. The crawfish they'd cleaned earlier had been mixed with vegetables and stuffed into a pot pie. Each of them got a hearty slice.

As if that wasn't enough, the Eggs Hussarde that came afterward was a truly special dish. It comprised a poached egg blanketed with hollandaise sauce and draped over bacon and mushrooms. The bacon and mushrooms had been soaked in their own rich, red wine sauce and all sat on top of an English muffin. To the side, there were large barbecued shrimp, browned with burnt sugar, alongside collard greens, okra cooked with crushed tomatoes, and potato casserole with melted cheese. A small ramekin filled with jalapeño shrimp cornbread completed the dish.

Roxy was so full from the earlier courses it took her a little time to get through this one, but she persevered because it was so delicious. As she ate, she listened to the sounds of friends enjoying themselves—the clink of glasses, the peals of laughter, the sounds of animated chatter.

Dessert followed, and once they were all done with their bread pudding in whiskey sauce, Evangeline clapped loudly. "Everyone, please listen," she said. Her expression and voice were serious, in sharp contrast to just a moment before. The place fell into silence.

"Now is the time," Evangeline said, "to hand over the ownership of my darlin' buildin'." She reached down into a bag that was under the table and pulled out a contract. Tears welled in her eyes. Then she coughed, pulled herself up straight and said, "No time for nonsense. We're here to do business. Louise, please join me, Cher."

Adrenaline pumped through Roxy's body. She looked at everyone at the table. They were all fixed on the scene between Evangeline and Louise. "I don't think you want to do that," Roxy said, her voice low.

"I don't?" Evangeline said.

Louise and Roxy's eyes locked for a moment. Louise squinted.

"What are you saying, honey?" she said. Louise's voice was low and syrupy sweet.

"I'm saying that there's more going on here than we truly know." Roxy didn't flinch under Louise's sharp gaze, but she was watchful. Louise, Evangeline's contract in her hand, was like a snake waiting to pounce.

"Hmmm, you're probably right. Evangeline, I think you'd better call the police," Louise said, her eyes still narrow and fixed on Roxy, her chin lifting. "I think we have a murderer in our midst."

"We certainly do," Roxy said. The atmosphere was tense. The two women seemed to be in a standoff, like a bull and a matador.

"What?" Evangeline was wild-eyed. "Who?"

There was silence, but then Louise dramatically swiveled her eyeballs to another part of the room. "Elijah!" she said. She looked down her nose at him in triumph.

"What?" Elijah said. He exploded out of his chair, his wiry frame shaking with adrenaline and indignation. "What are you talking about?"

"We should leave this to Detective Johnson," Sam said forcefully. "This is *not* our job."

"Huh," Louise scoffed. "You're probably in on it, too!" The giggly, flirty Louise of before had vanished.

Evangeline turned to Elijah, who was still on his feet. He was jiggling up and down with frustration. "Elijah, is this true, cher?"

"Of course it isn't!"

"Then why did you hide the fact that *you* were talking to Richard Lomas about selling your building?" Louise spat. "Did you think your secret would be safe forever?"

Evangeline gasped. Elijah crumpled back down to his seat and threw his head back, dragging his hands down his face. "Listen, I didn't tell you because I didn't want to influence your decision one way or another, Evangeline. And I didn't want to worry you. I was hoping to sell my building and move the bakery elsewhere in the city. But Lomas didn't offer me enough money, and I turned him down."

"But why didn't you tell us?" Evangeline cried. "We're your friends!"

Elijah looked embarrassed, "I thought you'd think badly of me for chasing the money and not protecting the buildings."

CHAPTER THIRTY-FOUR

"A LIKELY STORY," Louise scoffed.

Nat shook her head. "Elijah, how could you hide something like that from us?"

Roxy looked over at Sage whose eyes were closed. She looked peaceful, a small smile turning up the corners of her lips. Roxy wondered if she was meditating and had escaped to another place, maybe to a beautiful meadow where lambs were roaming free and butterflies fluttered over wildflowers.

But Roxy couldn't escape. She had to face reality. Terror of what she was about to do gripped her throat. Her hands trembled in her lap as she surreptitiously dialed 9-1-1 on her cell phone under the table.

"Look, I'm sorry for what I did, but I didn't *kill* anyone!" Elijah exclaimed.

Sam got up and put a strong arm around his shoulders. "Calm down, buddy." Then he faced the others and spoke firmly. "This has to stop, and it has to stop NOW. None of us knows what really happened. We're all jumping to conclusions and getting ourselves riled up. We should all go home and just go to bed. The police will sort it out."

"Ha!" Louise said, getting to her feet. "You think I can sleep at night?" She pointed at Elijah. "That *man* snuck into my room last night. He would have surely killed me if I hadn't been awake!"

"He was in your room?!" Nat said with a gasp.

"No, I wasn't!" Elijah looked as though his eyes would pop out of his head.

"No," Roxy said quietly. "He wasn't."

Louise looked confused. "But Roxy, you were there when . . ."

"When you *lied* to me," Roxy said.

"Huh?"

"Speak the truth, sweet love," said Sage, still not opening her eyes.

"I intend to." Roxy drew the card she had found in

the laundry from the pocket of her red dress and laid it on the table. "This is Louise's work ID card. Except your name isn't Louise, is it? It's Emma Warren."

Louise stood dead still, stunned.

"And you work for . . ." Roxy pointed to the card. "Tobin & Partners, a huge property development company in Dallas. I looked it up online."

"Lies!" Louise shouted.

Evangeline snatched the card up. "Let me see that."

Nat ran from her side of the table over to Evangeline. "Me too."

Roxy looked right at Louise. "You lied to me, to all of us. You were here all along to buy this guesthouse. You don't want to keep it and do it up nicely to preserve New Orleans heritage at all. You want to tear it down and build shiny new apartments, then sell them off for a huge profit, just like Richard Lomas wanted to."

Roxy felt a wave of anger run through her. "You tricked everyone. You made up all that stuff about your marriage failing, and that you were simply taking a break here. You pretended to be one of us. You lied and lied and lied. Even your name is made up! All for money. And then when Richard Lomas looked like he was going to beat you to a deal with Evangeline, you killed him. You lured him to the cemetery that night after the boat ride and shot him in cold blood.

"How could I have done that? I was drunk. Elijah had to escort me home."

"It was all a pretense. My guess is that Lomas told you he was negotiating with Elijah as well as Evangeline, and you seized your moment. You shot him *and* stole his phone so you could frame Elijah."

Suddenly, Louise recovered from her shock at being accused. She sneered. "All right. You're right about who I am, and that I wanted to get my hands on this guesthouse. But lying isn't a criminal offense. And you can't prove I killed Richard Lomas because I didn't."

Evangeline looked up at Louise, hate burning in her eyes. "Well, you're not gettin' this guesthouse now, let me tell you that. You're a liar and a cheat, and possibly a murderer, too."

Louise's face crumpled. She looked like she was in pain. She wandered away from the table toward the kitchen. "I felt *terrible* about lying to you. Not at first, but as it went on, and I could see you were all becoming *fond* of me." She let out a little sob. "I . . . I'm not sure I even want the guesthouse anymore."

Evangeline couldn't stop staring at Louise's ID while shaking her head. Then, quick as a flash, Louise darted into the kitchen.

"What's she doing?" Nat cried.

Evangeline got to her feet. "You get out of my kitchen!" She marched toward it, but before she could make it through the doorway, Louise was back.

She had gone into the kitchen tremulous and upset but now appeared completely deranged. Her eyes were wild and the whites of her eyes showed. Her hair was messed up, and she pulled at her sunshine yellow dress with her free hand like she wanted to rip it off. It was as though the exposure of her identity and motives had unhinged her completely. Everyone gasped. Louise had a huge carving knife in her hand.

CHAPTER THIRTY-FIVE

EVANGELINE, THE KNIFE a few inches from her chest, took a step back.

"You'll sign that contract, and you'll sign that contract now," Louise spat at her. "And no one here will *ever* say anything or contest this sale unless you want to end up like Richard Lomas. Six feet under."

"So you *did* kill him, then?" Roxy said.

Louise laughed. "Yes, Roxy, sweetie," she said in a cajoling voice. "I did."

"You're crazy, woman," Elijah said. "Give it up. You can't seriously think you're going to get away with this. We'll go to the police and tell them all about you. You'll be slammed in a cell by the end of the night."

"Hah! Not if you know what's good for you. Property development is a murderous, duplicitous industry of scum. It's teeming full of lowlifes, and I know most of them. They wouldn't think twice about picking you off one by one."

Evangeline's hands were trembling, but she kept her head high. "You will never *ever* get this guesthouse. Over my dead body."

"That can be arranged." Louise lunged, grabbed Evangeline, and held the carving knife in front of her. "Don't test me, old lady."

Sam, furious, barreled toward her. "STOP!"

"Don't move!" Louise said. "Nobody move!" She pressed the carving knife against Evangeline's straining neck. The elderly woman's veins bulged as did the one down the center of Louise's forehead. The atmosphere in the room was electric as the situation sat literally on a knife's edge. "We're not far from a really serious *accident* happening here."

Sam froze. Everyone did. Everyone except Nefertiti.

Unbeknownst to everyone, the fluffy white cat had silently padded downstairs. She brushed against Louise's leg, startling her. Louise flinched, and Sam, showing lightning reflexes, reached over and wrested the knife from her hand. As he did so, Roxy lunged at Louise as hard as she could. Despite Roxy's slight build, the force of her knocked Louise over. Roxy pinned her to the ground. Louise wasn't through yet, though. She wiggled and squirmed just like the crawfish Roxy and Nat had purged earlier. Roxy couldn't keep her down. Sam bent over to help, but Louise unleashed a mighty kick at his leg, and he doubled over in agony. As Roxy checked to see if Sam was okay, Louise twisted out of Roxy's grip and ran back into the kitchen. The gang of friends scurried after her.

Inside the white subway-tiled kitchen, Louise rushed over to the huge black range. She seized a 12-inch chef's knife from the counter. She waved it in front of her, threatening the group, the point of the gleaming knife glinting in the light. "Don't come near me!" she yelled. A lock of hair fell into her eyes, and she pushed it back roughly before grabbing a bottle of oil and pouring it into a nearby pan. With the knife shaking in her hand, she shouted, "If you're not going to give me the guesthouse, I'm going to burn it to the ground. Just you watch."

"No, don't!" Roxy screamed. She took a step forward. Louise thrust the knife toward her and grabbed her wrist, pulling her in. Now *Roxy* was being held hostage. Roxy could feel the edge of the knife against her skin.

"If any of y'all come near me, your darling Roxy will get it, do you hear?" Louise spat.

With her free hand, she got ahold of a lighter

and lit the gas burner. She placed the pan of oil on top. It shot up in flames. Louise cackled like a witch. She stood in front of the range, between the flames and the assembled group. "Now, we're all just going to have to wait, aren't we? Soon this wooden dump will be burned to the ground and maybe us along with it." She flashed an evil grin at Evangeline. "Insurance can't make up for lost heritage, can it?"

Louise was pressing the edge of the knife into Roxy so intently that she knew she couldn't move an inch. Louise wouldn't hesitate to harm her. Roxy didn't doubt Louise's words on that for a moment.

"Just give it up, Louise," Sam said in an authoritative voice.

She laughed at him, and casually leaned back against the edge of the range, her hand still holding the knife against Roxy's body. The flames were getting higher, the pan was starting to smoke.

Evangeline snorted. "You sick, sick woman."

Louise sneered. "You stupid, stupid woman. People like you deserve to get conned."

"You drop that knife right now, or I'll blast you into infinity." A voice boomed into the kitchen from outside.

"Detective Johnson!" Nat called out.

All the color drained from Louise's face, but she tightened her grip on Roxy. "Why should I?"

"It's over, Emma Warren," Johnson said, pushing through the kitchen door with his shoulder, gun cocked.

Louise began to laugh again, "Hahahahaha . . . aaaaargghhh!" She dropped the knife and pushed Roxy away from her. She half-turned from the range, slapping at her back. Her dress had caught on fire. Flames flickered from the bright yellow fabric at the back of her dress as it melted away, exposing Louise's reddened, hot flesh.

Sam, Elijah, and Nat lurched at her in unison, but Louise refused to submit that easily. Slapping her back with one hand, she tipped the oil onto the gas flame with the other. *Whooooosh!* A gigantic wall of fire shot into the air. The others raised their arms against the blanket of fearsome heat as Louise darted across the kitchen floor toward the back hallway, almighty crashes sounding as she pushed pots and pans to the ground behind her. She was running to the small back room where Nat and Roxy had purged the crawfish earlier.

"There's a back entrance there!" Evangeline hollered, grabbing a fire extinguisher. "Someone go round the outside, quick!"

Evangeline needn't have worried. Johnson's officers were already stationed there. A few moments later, a female police officer recited Louise her Miranda rights, while Louise screamed all kinds of expletives at her.

A silence settled over the six friends as they went to the front of the guesthouse to watch Louise being escorted into a waiting police car.

Elijah was sweating, red-faced, and angry, Sam looked nonplussed. Nat frowned, Evangeline's arms were crossed, while Sage stood serenely. Next to her, Roxy was quiet and thoughtful.

"Well, that's that taken care of," Johnson said as the cops shut the door on Louise. He turned to Roxy, looking slightly uncomfortable. "The tip-off you gave us this afternoon has led to a successful arrest."

Roxy brightened when he spoke. She grinned and dared to be a little bold. "Are you thanking me, Detective Johnson?"

Johnson was deadpan. "You have done your duty as a citizen."

"I'd take that as a yes!" Evangeline said. "It's the best you're gonna get!"

"What do you mean the tip-off?" Sam asked.

"I found Louise's real ID in the clothes I brought back from your laundry," Roxy said. "So I contacted Detective Johnson and set this little drama up. I hadn't anticipated she was going to turn quite so feral, though."

"Well, my trust issues just got much worse," Nat said with a sigh.

Sam looked at the detective. "Do you have enough evidence to charge her?"

"Per the plans we set up with Ms. Reinhardt this afternoon, we've got the confession recorded," Johnson said. "We'll search for the firearm used to commit the crime, and look for DNA evidence, but we've got plenty on her so far. Even if the murder case falls through, we could charge her with arson, attempted murder, you name it. She crossed a lot of lines back there. You were all in a lot of danger."

"Nonsense," Evangeline said. "Just a little skirmish, is all."

Johnson rolled his eyes. "Still as stubborn as ever, I see."

"Hurry up and search her room, would you? And get the heck out of my guesthouse," Evangeline said, shaking her head and flicking her hands as though Johnson were an insect whose presence on the premises wouldn't do Evangeline's reputation any good.

"Gladly," Johnson said drily.

CHAPTER THIRTY-SIX

LATER THAT NIGHT, Roxy was in her room with Nefertiti curled up on the bed beside her.

The day had been a rollercoaster. Her tarot card reading with Sage seemed like such a long time ago. Since then she'd argued with Sam in the laundry, spent the bulk of the day on her feet cooking, found the badge that clued her in to Louise's real identity, contacted Detective Johnson with her suspicions, confronted Louise at the dinner, wrestled her to the ground, had her life threatened, and watched a murderer get arrested.

And, after it all, she *still* didn't know where she would live, or what she would do. The case had been an excellent distraction, but now she had nothing to do, nothing to look forward to . . . no plans, no direction.

Exhausted, she had a little cry to let out all the tensions of the day, until there was a soft knock at her door. Roxy quickly wiped her tears and cleared her throat. "Come in," she croaked.

In came Evangeline, a look of concern on her face. She was followed by an equally serious-looking Sam.

"Oh," Roxy said, taken aback. She was sure she looked an absolute mess, her eyes ringed with mascara that had run, her red dress all crumpled and askew. "Hi." She tried to smooth out her hair and ran her fingertips under her eyes. Hopefully, the dim light hid the worst. "Sit down, go ahead."

Evangeline sat on the bed next to her while Sam dragged a chair over. "We've come with a proposition," Evangeline said.

"Okay . . .?" Roxy felt a little nervous.

"Don't look so scared," Sam said, with a gentle laugh. "It's nothing too terrible. At least, I hope not."

Evangeline spoke. Her green eyes were soft and gentle. "We've really enjoyed havin' you here, cher. You're a wonderful person, friendly but not too much, willin' to roll up your sleeves and get your hands dirty. And you solved the murder. That takes some moxie. I was goin' to ask you, well, I know you said you were startin' a new life. Do you . . . would you . . . will you become part-owner in this ole place with Sam and take over the day-to-day runnin' of the guesthouse from me?" Roxy's mind went into a spin.

"Nat'll stay on, of course," Evangeline said. "Sage'll do the website. I can even teach y'all how to *really* cook if you want. I can't stay forever, but I don't have to go rushin' off right away. Sam'll do the repairs and the laundry still, and Elijah'll bring all the bread and pastries, as usual."

Roxy stared at them. This couldn't be happening, could it? Something so good that was such a blessing? Things like this didn't happen to her. Life was a struggle!

"But I can't afford to buy it from you," she said.

"That's all right," Evangeline replied. "It's all settled. Sam's goin' to buy it and give you half. You'll be the manager with a steady paycheck and a stake in the property."

"Gosh." Roxy settled back onto the headboard and stared into space as she processed this information.

"Unless you have other plans, cher," Evangeline said gently. "I guess the world is your oyster now. You could go anywhere. Start afresh wherever you wanted."

"Though it'd be nice if you stuck around."

Sam's voice was deep and full of meaning. "Real nice."

Roxy looked up. Sam was looking right at her, his eyes sincere. She avoided them for a moment, pushing back the wave in her chest that was threatening to break. Instead, she pushed her fingers into Nefertiti's long fur and stroked her soft, soft belly.

Roxy allowed her thoughts to roam for a second or two. She imagined herself traveling out of New Orleans by bus, her bags packed, Nefertiti in her little carrier, as she rode away from all the new friends she had made. Where was she going? She didn't know. But as she imagined herself looking out of the window at this city she'd come to love, she felt a tug at her heart. Not a little tug, like a sentimental but necessary goodbye, but a gigantic pull, like someone had lassoed her with a thick rope and wasn't about to let go.

Her senses were alive. The colors of Mardi Gras flashed before her eyes and she heard the noises of the parades in her ears. She could smell the Cajun spices that lingered in the air around her like spirits urging her to stay. Perhaps *this* city, with all its magic and mystery and chaos was the place she'd finally make her home. It seemed so unlikely, but she had discovered that she was a little fiercer and a little wilder than she knew. New Orleans had brought all that moxie up to the surface.

"We'll give you some time to think about it, cher," Evangeline said, giving her a motherly pat on the knee.

"No," said Roxy.

She thought back to that wild, devil-may-care moment in her apartment. That split second when her spirit had told her,*WE'RE OFF!* no matter what her fearful mind countered with. This moment was different, though. The feeling didn't sweep over her from outside, gripping her soul with determination. This time, it bubbled up from somewhere deep within. To come to New Orleans had been a whim. To stay was a *conviction.*

Roxy looked Evangeline and Sam in the eyes and smiled. "I'm going to accept your offer with many thanks. I shall be delighted to stay."

CHAPTER THIRTY-SEVEN

TIME WHIZZED BY and before Roxy knew it, the night of the Grand Opening rolled around. She had changed the name of the guesthouse to the Funky Cat Inn, a nod to the jazz traditions of the city and the music she planned to provide regularly. She and Nat had spent weeks reimagining each room from scratch. They'd headed to the New Orleans Public Library and checked out numerous books on traditional buildings with pictures of sumptuous decors for inspiration.

They'd hit flea markets with Sam's laundry van (and his generous cash injection) and filled it up with all manner of French antiques and some amazing reproductions that they put to use in the communal and private rooms of the guesthouse.

Sam had also gotten to work. He had rewired the building and arranged all the structural repair work necessary. New windows had been installed and the balconies fixed. By the time he had finished, the Funky Cat Inn was up to code and then some.

On one of their trips to the flea market, Roxy finally broached the elephant in the room with Nat. "Where *does* Sam get all this money from? Surely the laundry business doesn't make enough for him to splash this amount of cash around?"

Nat raised her eyebrows. "We don't ask about that. I think he has family money, and he's a little embarrassed about it, but that's just a guess. Like I said, we don't talk about it."

"Why not?"

"He gets very cagey," Nat said. "So we don't push it. He grew up around here, his family goes way back, generations, and Evangeline always said that was good enough for her." That was the last they talked of it.

The dining room where tonight's event was to be held had been transformed. They'd split it into a grand lounge on one side, the dining area on the other. The whole place was painted a gorgeous, soft, pale blue. The room was now furnished with a mixture of champagne and pastel blue fabrics, mahogany side tables with ornately curved legs, lamps, gilded mirrors, and an abundance of interesting knickknacks and ornaments. They even had an enormous chandelier glittering overhead.

The bedrooms were sumptuous too, and Nefertiti looked more regal than ever curled up on one of the Louis-style four-poster beds. Her bright eyes matched the blue of the bedspreads exactly. She was the perfect accessory. Sage had taken a wonderful picture of her for their new Instagram page.

Sage had a great eye for photography. Her pictures of the food and the décor were so gorgeous that their social media follower counts were climbing every day. There had been a write-up in a local paper too, and slowly word was spreading that the Funky Cat Inn was the place to stay in New Orleans. Roxy trembled with anticipation when she thought about it.

Roxy felt she was in a permanent state of exhilaration. She had become so consumed by the whole process of turning the guesthouse from a vision in her head into a reality all around her that she often couldn't sleep. She'd never felt so accomplished.

"A boutique luxury, yet traditional, New Orleans experience" was the phrase she kept repeating to decorators, antique dealers, and just about anyone who would listen. It encapsulated precisely her goal for the new hotel.

Roxy rushed around on the day of the Grand Opening, but eventually, there was nothing more to do so she took herself to her room to get ready. She'd bought herself a new dress. She'd never have picked out something so show-stopping before, but being the new proprietor of this fabulous place and with some encouragement from Nat and Sage, she'd come to believe that a silver-sequined, figure-hugging dress wasn't *too* over the top. Okay, well maybe it was, especially when paired with an abundance of silver and crystal jewelry loaned to her by Sage and which now sparkled in her ears and around her neck and her wrists, but *why the heck not?* Wasn't life for enjoying, after all?

They were expecting a big turnout, but Roxy couldn't help drumming her fingertips on the arm of one of the couches as she finally sat down and waited for her guests to arrive. The time seemed to tick by so, so slowly. They'd printed flyers and passed them out just about everywhere. Elijah had distributed them with every beignet purchase made at his bakery, Sam had wrapped one inside every laundry parcel, Sage had left a whole bunch at the botanica, and Nat had spent all her days off on the street at the end of the alleyway handing out details of the event to passersby.

They'd even sent an invitation to Mara Lomas, a kind of peace offering. After Louise had been arrested, Mara had come back around to the guesthouse in tears, saying to them how ashamed she was of her behavior. They'd tried to console her by telling her that she had been right—it *was* one of them who had killed her husband—but the message didn't seem to get through. Mara was determined to feel guilty and she had returned to her home state to make some sense of her life. Roxy didn't expect Mara to attend the Grand Opening, but she'd written on the invitation, "We wish you all the best for the future," and she really did.

Nat came and sat next to Roxy. She patted her on the shoulder. Roxy wouldn't have dreamed of asking her to drop her "uniform," but Nat herself had said, "With all this grandeur, I feel a little silly in my Slipknot tee. Slipknot's a band by the way," she added to relieve Roxy of her perplexed expression. Instead, Nat was wearing a smart, tailored trouser suit that looked awesome on her. She'd paired it with her shiny green boots with the sparkly laces, which somehow worked, and a plain white T-shirt. Her ears continued to drip with jewelry, and she had kept her tiny diamond nose stud in place. "So that I still feel like myself," she'd said.

Shortly after 6 PM, people began to trickle in. Evangeline, who had helped with the food, handed the guests glasses of wine and Café Brûlot. The tables were laid out with what seemed like thousands of New Orleans-style canapés, and Sage offered tarot readings in the lounge.

Elijah and Sam were on the music, filling the whole place with warm jazz and the cool, mellow sounds of Miles Davis along with the more upbeat tunes of Duke Ellington, filtered through the air. After a while, Nat joined them, astounding Roxy as she demonstrated the most beautiful, soulful voice Roxy had ever heard. Nat sung jazz classics, *Smoke Gets In Your Eyes,* and *It Don't Mean A Thing If It Ain't Got That Swing* and then, with a level of graciousness that she had not previously been known for, she took song requests from Roxy's guests.

As they finished a set, Roxy walked up to her. "Why didn't you tell me you could sing?" she whispered.

"Ah, it's nothing," Nat said, shyly.

"Nothing? You were fantastic!"

"Nat only gets her voice out on special occasions," Sam said. "For *special* people," he added.

"When she sings, she has a true Southern vibe," Sage said. She raised her eyebrows. "Quite unusual when you consider she's from across the pond."

CHAPTER THIRTY-EIGHT

LATER THAT EVENING, Roxy felt like a break and stepped outside into the warm night air. The stars were all out, and it seemed like even they were smiling down at her.

She found Sam out there too, his back turned to her as he looked up to the sky.

"Oh, hey," she said.

He jumped. "Hi, Roxy." He grinned. "Going great, isn't it?"

"Yep!"

"The stars are all out in celebration," he said.

"Lovely clear night, isn't it?" They gazed up at the stars for a moment in companionable silence. "You were wrong about New Orleans, you know," she said eventually. "It *is* magic."

Sam cleared his throat. "I've been meaning to say this for a while." He stared at his feet. "But you know, dumb male pride and all."

Roxy stayed silent and watched him.

"I don't think I spoke to you very nicely when you came to the laundry, when you talked about your suspicions concerning Elijah."

Roxy had let that go a long time back. She laughed. "Well, you *were* right. It wasn't him, and at that point, it really would have been wise for me to butt out. It was only after we spoke that I found Louise's badge and got a part to play."

Sam looked down at her. "That's all true. But I could have spoken in more of a polite manner."

"Ever the Southern gentleman," Roxy said fondly. "Well, that means I'll have to be a *proper Southern belle.*" She tried to put on the accent and failed miserably. They both burst into laughter.

Roxy didn't quite know what came over her. Maybe it was the champagne, or the beauty of the stars, or the deep happiness she felt in her soul, but she wanted to reach out and kiss him. She paused, though, wondering if it were appropriate. Would he kiss her back? Would he jump away and be like, "You've got the wrong idea! We're business partners, that's all!"? Her hesitation broke the spell, and she gave him an awkward smile instead. The doubts she had about him came flooding back. Perhaps those red flags meant something. Maybe he was just pretending to be a nice guy.

At that moment, Nat came bustling around the corner. "Roxy, I've been looking . . ." She cut herself short. "Ooooh," she said, her eyes shining. "Have I interrupted something?"

"No!" Roxy said a little too forcefully.

Nat raised an eyebrow. "If you say so. Anyway, come on inside. We're all waiting for you, Rox."

It was coming up on midnight. Inside, everyone had a champagne glass in hand, and there was a round of applause when Roxy made her way back in.

"Evangeline was just saying how proud she was of you, how you've transformed the place," Nat said. "They want to hear something from you now."

Roxy would have *died* in her former life if she'd had to do any form of public speaking. But now, here, considering who she was in this moment, all her nerves fell away, and she was filled with a deep sense of warmth and affection.

"Thank you all for coming," she said. "This place . . . it has come to mean so much to me. Not just this guesthouse, but the whole city. New Orleans is full of magic and wonder. It has changed me. When I got here, I had no idea where my life would lead. I had nothing except my suitcase full of clothes and my cat. No job. No family. No one by my side. No direction. I was painfully shy and didn't have any sort of belief in myself. But . . . this city has changed me. It has taught me that miracles do happen, that I have a power inside me that I've never been aware of. I'm a new person now, a better person, a more empowered person. And, thanks to your amazing cuisine, also a slightly fatter person!" Everyone laughed.

"So I just want to say thank you. Thank you to Evangeline for introducing me to Creole and Cajun ways. Thank you to Nat, the craziest, most loveable girl I know. Thank you to Sage, for making me believe in magic. Thank you to Elijah, for showing me that it's okay to be different and that beignets are food from the heavens. Thank you to Sam, for being . . . a great friend. And thank you to New Orleans for helping me find myself. I am beyond grateful for this new chapter in my life." She raised the glass of champagne that Nat had thrust into her hand. "And thank you for being here to share it with me."

The crowd applauded, and Roxy looked around. The dining room was full of people, chattering, laughing, eating and drinking. She wandered into the lobby where she could survey the entire room. As she watched the scene in front of her, she felt a huge sense of satisfaction and achievement.

"I *did* this," she whispered to herself. She almost couldn't believe it.

Her phone gave a little "ting." She looked at the screen. There was a text from Angela, her call center supervisor at Modal Appliances, Inc.

`Jade and Chloe have been fired for fighting in the women's bathroom. We are two customer service reps down. Come back to work at 9 AM sharp, but no pay for the time you missed. Don't be late!`

Roxy read the text several times. She tapped out a reply.

`Can't make it. Sorry. Good luck, though.`

She looked back at the room and watched her guests. Sam waved from across the room.

She knew what to do. She didn't hesitate. There was no grief, no loss, no love lost. She swiped her phone. There was a "whoosh." Angela was gone for good.

Thank you for reading *Mardi Gras Madness (Large Print Edition)*! I hope you love Roxy and her gang as

much as I do. The next book in the Roxy series continues her story as she finds herself in the midst of yet more mayhem.

A New Orleans guesthouse. A social media murder. A killer with a virtual ax to grind . . .

Can Roxy reveal the killer before they strike again? Or is her reputation dead on arrival? Follow the link below to get your copy of *New Orleans Nightmare* (*Large Print Edition*) from Amazon!

https://www.alisongolden.com/new-orleans-nightmare-paperback-large-print.

To find out about new books, sign up for my newsletter: https://www.alisongolden.com.

If you love the Inspector Graham mysteries, you'll also love the sweet, funny *USA Today* best-selling Reverend Annabelle Dixon series featuring a madcap, lovable lady vicar whose passion for cake is matched only by her desire for justice. Follow the link below to get your copy of *Death at the Café* (*Large Print Edition*) from Amazon!

https://www.al

isongolden.com/ death-at-the-cafe-pa perback-large-print

If you love the Reverend Annabelle series, you'll want to read the *USA Today* bestselling Inspector Graham series featuring a new and unusual detective with a phenomenal memory and a tragic past. Follow the link below to get your copy of *The Case of the Screaming Beauty* (*Large Print Edition*) from Amazon!

https://www.al isongolden.com/ screaming-beauty-pa perback-large-print

If you're looking for something edgy and dangerous, root for Diana Hunter as she seeks justice after a devastating crime destroys her family. Start following her journey in this non-stop series of suspense and action. Follow the link below to get your copy of *Snatched* (*Large Print Edition*) from Amazon!

https://www.al

isongolden.com/ snatched-paperback-large-print

I hugely appreciate your help in spreading the word about *Mardi Gras Madness*, including telling a friend. Reviews help readers find books! Please leave a review on your favorite book site.

Turn the page for an excerpt from the next book in the Roxy Reinhardt series, *New Orleans Nightmare . . .*

A ROXY REINHARDT MYSTERY

NEW ORLEANS NIGHTMARE

LARGE PRINT EDITION

USA TODAY BESTSELLING AUTHOR

ALISON GOLDEN WITH HONEY BROUSSARD

NEW ORLEANS NIGHTMARE

CHAPTER ONE

"OOOOH, I'M SO excited!" Roxy Reinhardt said, dancing around the kitchen, while pots and pans of all sizes bubbled on the stovetop. Gumbos, stews, and jambalayas filled the room with rich, spicy steam as she boogied in the space between the range and the countertops.

"Me too!" Nat said, clapping her hands together.

Roxy was the manager and part-owner of the Funky Cat Inn, having been recently installed as such by the previous owner, Evangeline, and local investor, laundryman, handyman, and something of a handsome dark horse, Sam. Nat was Roxy's "Girl Friday." She was also a former English nanny who had overstayed her visa. Today they were preparing a "Grand Welcome Meal."

"Who are these people again?" Evangeline asked Roxy, for the third time. "I don't understand all these new-fangled Instabook things, cher."

Evangeline was retired and living her own life now, but she still came over to help them with the food. She was an absolute master at Creole and Cajun cooking and baking, and Roxy and Nat had submitted themselves to an extended tutelage.

"They're called influencers," Roxy explained. "That means that they have a lot of followers on Instagram."

"Huh?" Evangeline said.

Nat rolled her eyes and gave Roxy a wink as she looked back from a pot of gumbo she was stirring. "Instagram is a platform where you have your own page, and you put pictures on it. If people like what they see, they follow you to watch what you're going to put up next. We have a page for the Funky Cat. Sage runs it."

"So why are these . . ." Evangeline frowned. "Why are these influgrammers comin' here?"

"*Influencers,* Evangeline," Nat said.

Roxy laughed. "Influgrammers sounds pretty good, though! You might have just coined a new word there, Evangeline. Anyway, the influencers are coming here to stay as part of a promotion. We pay them to showcase their visit. All the pictures and videos they shoot while they are here get put on their Instagram feed, and their followers will see them. Since they have hundreds of thousands of followers, it's great publicity. This is huge for us."

Roxy had arrived in New Orleans during Mardi Gras season. Now though, spring had brightened into summer and the vivid colors and excitement of Mardi Gras were over. The city had lazily tilted into June, but with the imminent arrival of the influencers, the atmosphere at the Funky Cat was ramping up to a level never experienced in the building's entire 102-year existence.

Evangeline sighed, shaking her head with bemusement. "Back in my day, people simply bought an ad in a magazine or two."

Well into her eighties, Evangeline bustled around the kitchen with pots and spices, her floral wraparound dresses swishing beneath her aprons as she did so. She was a flurry of bustle and action. She could still manage six pans on the flame at one time, and ordered Roxy and Nat about the place as if she still owned the kitchen, which, when she was in it, she did.

Nat picked up a large sack of crawfish and carried it into the back room to begin purging them. "Times have changed, Evangeline, and we've gotta keep up if we want the Funky Cat to be a success."

"It only has six rooms!" Evangeline cried, rearranging bags of spices on the counter. "How much of a success can it be?"

Roxy felt awkward. She didn't want to talk about how much more upscale the boutique hotel was now or how expensive the rooms had become since Evangeline's time as owner; it would be rude and embarrassing.

"Well, the room rates are just a touch higher, so we need a new, more affluent demographic, that's all. Now, shouldn't we get started on the jalapeño cornbreads? Where have those ramekins gotten to?"

They were really going to town on the welcome meal for the influencers. It was to be a five-course affair.

"Do you think they'll be able to eat all this lot?" Nat wondered out loud as she wandered back into the kitchen a few minutes later. She was carrying a pot of newly purged crawfish with a grin on her face. "For course one, we've got a chicken gumbo with Cajun spices." Nat ladled up a spoonful of the gumbo and let it slowly pour back into the pan. "Followed by miniature crawfish and cheese pies, followed by Shrimp Creole. That's shrimp cooked in tomatoes, peppers and hot sauce, with white rice, Roxy," the young English woman said gravely.

Nat was a Funky Cat treasure. She helped Roxy with anything that was needed at the boutique hotel, from cooking to serving guests, from checking them in to cleaning their rooms. And her talents extended even further. Nat possessed a voice that was so smooth and creamy that Roxy had hired her on the spot to sing for guests.

Now, Nat's black nail polish gleamed in the lights of the kitchen. Her excitement about the upcoming meal really *was* something. Getting the cynical, skeptical Nat to be joyous and upbeat about anything was a true feat. But then, what was coming was a bold, new experiment for the small hotel.

"Yum, and I'm preparing dessert—warm bread pudding with caramel and whiskey sauce," Roxy said.

"Don't forget the cheese course!" Evangeline cried out from where she was stirring a huge pot of broth.

"I'm not sure they will be able to eat it all, but I do know that thousands and thousands will be watching via their Instagram accounts, and we have to give a great impression, not only of the Funky Cat, but of New Orleans," Roxy finished.

The city was the first place Roxy had ever felt truly at home. It was hard to explain, but New Orleans had gotten into her bones somehow. There was a *heat* about "N'awlins" as the locals called it, perhaps from the spices, perhaps from the carnivals and the magic and the spiritualism that lurked about the place, perhaps from the music that floated from basements and businesses at any time of the day or night. Whatever it was, the essence of it had found its way into Roxy's very soul, lodged itself there, and wasn't about to leave any time soon.

As she chopped onions and garlic for the Shrimp Creole, Roxy sighed happily to herself. Things were *finally* falling into place in her life, and she felt cozy and warm and safe. Just then, they heard the sound of the front door knocker being rapped. Hard.

Roxy frowned, her knife paused over an onion. She was expecting Sam, but he'd have simply walked in without knocking. Roxy wiped her hands down her apron and hurried out of the kitchen, through the dining room and into the hallway. The influencers weren't due for a good three hours. She hoped this wasn't one of them arriving early. She wanted to be dressed in her best and have the food ready before they got even so much as a glimpse of the Funky Cat or its proprietor. A little flustered, she pulled open the door. Her heart sank.

A very tall, slim woman with huge sunglasses and long, black hair that cascaded in waves down her back stood on the doorstep. She wore chunky high heels on her feet, skinny jeans, and a leather jacket with a fur collar that looked very expensive indeed. Behind her, six Louis Vuitton suitcases and two holdalls were piled up in the courtyard. Without so much as a greeting, the woman walked assuredly past Roxy and into the Funky Cat lobby.

"Oh, hello," Roxy said, stepping back to give the woman room to pass. *Who was she?* The woman had walked in like *she* owned the place, a demeanor that Roxy suspected was her visitor's default setting. Then she remembered who the woman was!

"Good afternoon," the visitor said, pushing her sunglasses on top of her head. "I am Ada Okafor." The woman eyed Roxy. "But I expect you knew that. I'm early, I know. I'm always early. The early bird catches the worm. Snooze, you lose." She flicked her wrist and poked one forefinger into the air.

Roxy recovered quickly. "Great to meet you. I'm Roxy Reinhardt, part-owner and manager of this hotel." Roxy stuck out her hand, but Ada didn't seem to notice so Roxy gestured down at her apron, embarrassed. "Yes, um, I'm afraid we aren't quite, um, ready for the grand welcome we wanted to give you." What was happening to her? All Roxy's confidence and excitement had evaporated at the sight of this officious, elegant woman.

"It's fine," Ada said, though her mouth twitched. She didn't look impressed. "I will go to my room and do some editing on the mag while you," she looked Roxy up and down, "pull yourself together." Ada Okafor ran a travel magazine for rich Nigerians who wanted to jet-set around the world like she did. She had a huge international following on Instagram in the luxury travel market.

Ada looked around. "But who will carry my bags?"

To get your copy of *New Orleans Nightmare* (*Large Print Edition*) visit the link below:

https://www.alisongolden.com/new-orleans-nightmare-paperback-large-print

"Your emails seem to come on days when I need to read them because they are so upbeat."
- Linda W -

For a limited time, you can get the first books in each of my series - *Chaos in Cambridge, Hunted* (exclusively for subscribers - not available anywhere else), *The Case of the Screaming Beauty, and Mardi Gras Madness* - plus updates about new releases, promotions, and other Insider exclusives, by signing up for my mailing list at:

https://www.alisongolden.com/roxy

TAKE MY QUIZ

What kind of mystery reader are you?
Take my thirty second quiz to find out!

https://www.alisongolden.com/quiz

BOOKS IN THE ROXY REINHARDT MYSTERIES

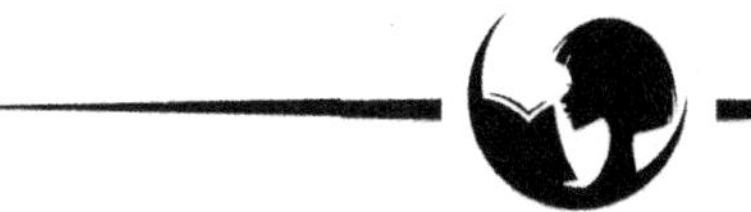

Visit the link below for all my large print editions ***www.alisongolden.com/large-print***

Mardi Gras Madness

New Orleans Nightmare

Louisiana Lies

Cajun Catastrophe

COLLECTIONS

(regular print only)

Books 1-3

Mardi Gras Madness

New Orleans Nightmare

Louisiana Lies

ALSO BY ALISON GOLDEN

Visit the link below for all my large print editions:

www.alisongolden.com/large-print

FEATURING INSPECTOR DAVID GRAHAM

The Case of the Screaming Beauty

The Case of the Hidden Flame

The Case of the Fallen Hero

The Case of the Broken Doll

The Case of the Missing Letter

The Case of the Pretty Lady

The Case of the Forsaken Child

The Case of Sampson's Leap

The Case of the Uncommon Witness

FEATURING REVEREND ANNABELLE DIXON

Chaos in Cambridge (Prequel)

Death at the Café

Murder at the Mansion

Body in the Woods

Grave in the Garage

Horror in the Highlands

Killer at the Cult

Fireworks in France

Witches at the Wedding

As A. J. Golden

FEATURING DIANA HUNTER

Hunted (Prequel)

Snatched

Stolen

Chopped

Exposed

ABOUT THE AUTHOR

Alison Golden is the *USA Today* bestselling author of the Inspector David Graham mysteries, a traditional British detective series, and two cozy mystery series featuring main characters Reverend Annabelle Dixon and Roxy Reinhardt. As A. J. Golden, she writes the Diana Hunter thriller series.

Alison was raised in Bedfordshire, England. Her aim is to write stories that are designed to entertain, amuse, and calm. Her approach is to combine creative ideas with excellent writing and edit, edit, edit. Alison's mission is simple: To write excellent books that have readers clamouring for more.

Alison is based in the San Francisco Bay Area with her husband and twin sons. She splits her time between London and San Francisco.

For up-to-date promotions and release dates of upcoming books, sign up for the latest news here: https://www.alisongolden.com/roxy.

For more information:
www.alisongolden.com
alison@alisongolden.com

facebook.com/alisongolden.books
x.com/alisonjgolden
instagram.com/alisonjgolden

THANK YOU

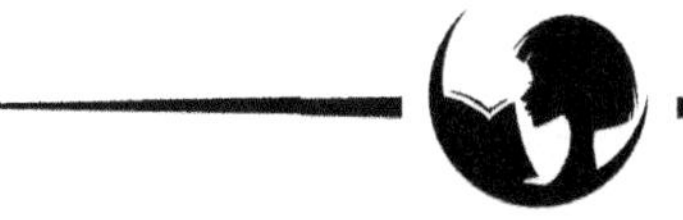

Thank you for taking the time to read *Mardi Gras Madness*. If you enjoyed it, please consider telling your friends or posting a short review. Word of mouth is an author's best friend and very much appreciated.

Thank you,

Alison

Printed in Great Britain
by Amazon